LONGARM'S NO FOOL...

At closer range the rifleman was young and rat-faced, with a week's growth of beard and army pants. It was a dragoon outfit, judging from the paler blue stripes down the legs. From the waist up, he wore an undershirt and had a dire need for soap and water. "Our squaw can tend to your critters," he said. "What was that name again?"

"Washington," Longarm lied, "Booker T. Washington."

–• TABOR EVANS •–

LONGARM

ON THE
SIWASH TRAIL

A JOVE BOOK

LONGARM ON THE SIWASH TRAIL

A Jove Book/published by arrangement with
the author

PRINTING HISTORY
Jove edition/September 1986

ISBN: 0-515-08675-4

Jove Books are published by The Berkley Publishing Group,
200 Madison Avenue, New York, N.Y. 10016. The words
"A JOVE BOOK" and the "J" with sunburst are trademarks
belonging to Jove Publications, Inc.

LONGARM

ON THE
SIWASH TRAIL

Chapter 1

The desert sun was just rising, so Town Constable Bull Culhane was just fixing to lie down when one of his deputies came in and announced soberly, "Stranger just rid in off the salt flats. Says he's looking for you specific, Bull. I sent him to the Silver Spur instead. He says he's law, too. But he looks more like a Danite to me, and you know how them fool Avenging Angels confuse our brand of law with the Book of Mormon."

The gray and weathered senior lawman didn't answer as he rose from the cot to reach for his hat and gun rig. He knew for sure he would need the hat, now that the sun was up, on the warm side of the Fourth of July. He hoped he wouldn't need either of the guns he was strapping on. The tough little mining town of Rosebud Wash was a mite far west of Mormon country, and the Salt Lake Temple had disowned the Danite extremists in any case since the army had hanged Brother Lee. But as he headed for the back door of the lockup, Culhane told his deputy to go wake the day watch.

His younger sidekick nodded. "We'll be there with bells and guns on to back your play, Bull," he said. "But don't you mean to wait till we're set to do so?"

Culhane shook his head and answered, "It's neither neighborly nor sensible to bust in on a gent at the head of an armed posse afore you hear the tale he has to tell. He asked for me polite, so I mean to meet him the same way."

He reached for the door latch. "How come you wants the whole force alerted if you ain't expecting trouble, then?" his deputy asked.

"To make sure you're all alerted, of course," the older and wiser lawman said. "If he takes me, wide awake, I hates to consider what he might do to a mess of sleeping beauties."

Before his deputy could answer, Culhane was outside in the alley. The cobweb-dry desert air was still cool in the shade, so Culhane hugged such shade as there might be as he eased down the alley, his chest feeling a mite tight. He forced himself to breathe deeply and told his heart not to act so foolish. His brain and his gun hand had kept it beating nigh sixty years, and this wasn't the first time a mysterious stranger had called an unexpected meeting. Nine times out of ten such conversations ended friendly. Culhane had lived through the other kinds by taking such precautions as arriving via the unexpected route.

2

The back door of the town livery was closer to the lockup than the saloon was. Culhane ducked in there and moved between the stalls to where he found Greaser Bill lounging in the wider street entrance and said, "Morning, Greaser Bill."

The fat Mexican seated on a nail keg was almost startled enough to rise. *"Madre de Dios,* Bull. For why do I find you in my stalls with the other jackasses this morning?" he asked.

"I hear a stranger just rode in," Culhane said. "Unless he's cruel as hell to animals he must have left his pony here with you, right?"

Greaser Bill chuckled and replied, "Wrong. He came in aboard one Spanish mule, leading another. He is an hombre who knows much about the Great Basin in high summer. He rides an army saddle and wears low-heeled army boots. His saddle gun is a Winchester .44-40. He took it with him after he helped me unsaddle his brutes and rub them down. I could not help noticing he carries a Colt .44, double-action, in a cross-draw rig under the frock coat of his tenderfoot suit. I did not ask him whether he was a preacher or a gambling man. He was most polite, but not the sort of hombre one feels free to annoy after a long, hard ride."

"Wes said he looked hardcased. Did he tell you where he rid in from, Greaser Bill?"

The Mexican shook his head, but said, "There is only one place he could have come from, at this time of the year. The nearest fresh water is down at Rye Patch, on the Humbolt, no?"

Culhane nodded thoughtfully. "Might make more sense to *ask* him than to stand here guessing."

He turned and moved back through the stalls. It

would have been closer just to pop out the damned front and make for the nearby front entrance of the saloon. But Culhane had promised his heart he'd never do that again after taking a bullet through a lung in Elko one night while trying to save a few extra steps.

It was getting warmer now. Culhane would have been sweating by the time he reached the back door of the Silver Spur if the thirsty desert air let sweat bead on a man's face. He mounted the sun-silvered steps on the balls of his booted feet and went in. The hallway between the kitchen and the back rooms was cooler and darker. Culhane eased to the beaded curtain at the business end of the corridor and peered soberly through it. The main room of the Silver Spur was empty, save for the barkeep and a dusty but soberly dressed stranger seated in a far corner at a table with a schooner of beer. The barkeep was wiping the mahogany, not looking proddy, even though he had taken down the mirror behind the bar.

The stranger was somewhere on the comfortable side of forty and dark enough to pass for an Indian or at least a breed if he hadn't had a heroic moustache and ruggedly handsome Anglo-Saxon features. He was smoking a three-for-a-nickel cheroot the same color as his pancaked Stetson and tweed suit. The Winchester Greaser Bill had mentioned was on the table inside the reach of the beer schooner. As Culhane watched, the stranger loosened the knot of his shoestring tie and unbuttoned the top button of his hickory shirt. He reached into his vest pocket to take out a railroad watch and called it an awful name.

Culhane took a deep breath and stepped through the beaded curtain. The stranger didn't go for his artillery.

He just looked up with a scowl and growled, "I surely hope you'd be Constable Culhane. For if you ain't, he's surely taking his own sweet time this morning."

"I'm Culhane," the town law said. "For openers, there's a town ordinance against drinking with firearms on the table in this town. Your turn."

"I ain't drinking with my saddle gun," the stranger said. "But it would be lawful if I wanted to. For I'm law, too. Federal. I'm Deputy U. S. Marshal Custis Long. I generally ride for the Denver District Court under U. S. Marshal Billy Vail. I'd show you my I.D. if you didn't look so armed and unsettled. Why don't we both get some beer and our hands on this same table, polite, so's I can conduct this courtesy call more courteous?"

Culhane laughed with sick relief and said, "Jesus Christ, Billy Vail might have wired me you was coming. You just scared me wide awake after a night on duty."

He signaled the barkeep for some additional suds as he strode over to sit down. "I knows Billy Vail of old. You must be the one they calls Longarm, right?" he asked.

Longarm shrugged modestly. "It beats being called Custis. Billy told me about you, too. Said to make sure I dropped in on you before making any noise in your territory, Bull. Is it true you once shot a Texas Ranger in Virginia City?"

Culhane looked defensive as he replied, "Hell, how was I to know he was law when I seen him throw down on a leading citizen of the community? Pimps has rights, too, and had Texas tolt me they wanted the son of a bitch I'd have been proud to arrest him for her. But let's not discuss my misspent youth, Longarm. What in thunder is a Colorado lawman doing out here in the Great Basin, so far from home?"

Longarm replied, "Billy Vail ain't sure, and I sure wish they'd let me stop. The State Department borrowed me off Justice to ride herd on distinguished foreigner with a hunting license."

He paused while the barkeep placed a schooner between them for Culhane. Then he continued, "The tale of woe begins in Vienna town, where a printer named Krinke seems to have took it into his head he'd get rich quicker if he just produced his own Austro–Hungarian paper money and cut out all the middle men. But the Emperor Franz Josef has laws even more ferocious than our own about counterfeiting."

"Ain't old Franz Josef kin to that Emperor Max, down Mexico way?" Culhane asked. "The one old Juarez shot?"

Longarm nodded. "He was an unemployed younger prince or something. Nobody ever accused the Hapsburgs of being smart. But even an idiot emperor can see the disadvantages of letting subjects print their own money. Washington can, too. The wayward printer lit out for the Land of the Free as the Austro–Hungarian law was closing in. But when he tried to claim political asylum they told him not to be silly and held him for his own government."

Longarm helped himself to a sip of beer before he went on. "While a peace officer from Vienna town was crossing the pond to take Krinke off our hands, he busted out of the Washington lockup and was last seen headed west, no doubt to seek life, liberty, and a place to set up shop again. The Treasury Department wants

6

him caught as well. But after that it gets complicated. They never got around to taking pictures of the rascal in Washington and he describes as nondescript. The only man who knows him by sight is the man I'm looking for. He's called Herr Oberst Von Thaldorf. An oberst is a full colonel. They must want him worse than we do."

Culhane lowered his own schooner, considerably depleted, and asked, "Can we get to the part about you being here in Rosebud Wash, now?"

"I figured it was obvious. When Von Thaldorf traced Krinke as far west as Salt Lake City, the State Department began to worry about *him* getting lost, robbed, or worse. So, recalling that I knew the country better, they sent me from Denver to join the posse of one before it vanished into the desert. But by the time I reached Salt Lake it already had. The infernal colonel left word at his hotel he'd heard Krinke was in Nevada, saying awful things about Franz Josef. So he wanted me to meet him in Rye Patch."

"I take it you never did?"

"You take it right. Time I got off at Rye Patch, with a brace of mules from Fort Douglas and some sensible desert gear, the colonel had checked out of the only hotel in town. He left me a message saying a Hungarian dwelling in Rye Patch for some fool reason had told him Krinke had been seen boarding the stage for Rosebud Wash, and that he meant to follow."

Longarm drained the last of his own beer, put down the empty schooner and said, "So here we are. Neither the stage nor the Western Union wires extend a mile farther out into nothing much. By now you'd have told me if you'd seen either of the gents, and it ain't as if this is a vast metropolis to lose oneself in, no offense.

7

"They tell me this is the only saloon and that there ain't no hotels. I'm out of ideas and open to suggestions, Bull."

Culhane finished his own beer and signaled for two more, but the younger lawman shook his head. "You go ahead. I like to pace myself on duty."

Culhane nodded and pulled in one finger. "I feels for you, but I just can't reach you, Longarm. I'd recall *one* such furriner, let alone two, if either was skulking about our fair city. There ain't five hundred living souls in the entire township, and I knows 'em all on sight. As you may have noticed, the country all around is dead flat sage or salt flat. The only bump in the earth worth mention is the silver reef a mile up the wash, and the mines is too played out to be hiring. I could ask, however."

Longarm shook his head and said, "I already did. A hard-rock man on his way home from the diggings stopped in here just before you did, and it only cost me a beer to determine nobody's been hired or shooting guns up that way."

"They ain't here, then. What if that outlaw come up here, saw he'd boxed hisself at the end of the line, and doubled back aboard the same stage?"

"That would account for Krinke not being here," Longarm said. "But Colonel Thaldorf is still left over. He ain't in Rye Patch. He ain't here. He ain't stretched out by the trail anywhere between. So what's left?"

Culhane agreed it was a pure mystery. Then he brightened and said, "Hold on, Longarm. I got a wild notion that just might work."

He took some time to compose his thoughts as Longarm waited. Then he said, "We did have some strangers passing through the day afore yesterday. Does that fit your timetable?"

Longarm nodded. Culhane went on, "It was an emigrant train, bound for the Oregon apple country via the Siwash Trail. About a dozen families and as many covered wagons. Now that I study on it, there was so many of 'em a nondescripted furriner could have been mixed in, and who would have noticed?"

Longarm glanced out through the grimy window. He frowned and asked, "Who in thunder would be headed out across open desert in covered wagons at this time of the year, Bull?"

The older lawman said, "I told you, emigrants, bound for Oregon by way of the Siwash Trail. It's a cutoff, laid out during the Paiute troubles a few years back. As you know, the Iron Horse has replaced most of the old overland routes. But the Willamette Valley of Oregon is still a place you has to get to the hard way at least part way. Them settlers unloaded their wagons at Rye Patch, where the rails swing southwest for California. They followed the stage line this far and then, no matter how we argued, headed out to the northwest along the Siwash Trail for Fort Bidwell. If they make it, there's water and grass enough to matter from there on to the promised land. What if that owlhoot from Austria joined up with 'em?"

Longarm shrugged and said, "A wagon party's always glad to have an extra gunhand along. But we got a leftover Austrian colonel."

Culhane nodded. "If he arrived at night aboard yet another stage, or even riding, I could have missed him, just passing through. I can't be everywhere at once, you know. What say your greenhorn lawman showed up just after that wagon train left, put two and two together as smart as us, and lit out after 'em? That surely would explain neither one being here or back at the railroad, right?"

Longarm stubbed out his smoked-down cheroot, lit another, and said, "Tell me some more about this Siwash Trail. I never heard of it and, no offense, I was out here during the Paiute troubles. I'd likely *still* be out here, had not Princess Winnemucca married white and talked her people into behaving better. Scouting desert Indians in the desert can sure add up to wasted effort."

Culhane nodded and said, "Paiute don't fight as dirty as Apache, but they's twice as sneaky. And it smarts to get hit with an arrow when your own eyes and common sense tells you there can't *be* any Injuns for as far as one can see across dead-flat nothing-much. It was during the Paiute troubles the Siwash Trail was laid out. That is to say, folk aiming to get to Fort Bidwell without going through the Paiute country to the southwest took the suggestions of the Siwash Injun who first found the passage across hitherto unexplored and doubtless suicidal empty space on the ordinance maps."

Longarm frowned. "Back up, bull. There's no such critter as a Siwash Indian. Siwash is a dirty word in Chinook trade jargon. When a Chinook calls another a Siwash he's looking for a fight. And, besides, we're a mite south of Chinook country."

Culhane nodded. "I know. The old Injun *said* he'd come down from the northwest. I wasn't here at the time. I was on the force at Elko when the old gent rid in one night with a couple of arrows in his back. But the way I hear it, the folk here at the time treated him

Christian, considering, and as he lay dying he tolt 'em he'd made it almost down from Fort Bidwell afore someone arrowed him for reasons only another Injun might savvy. The arrows was Paiute, so it stands to reason the old Injun had to be something else. The local business interests paying for his bandages and firewater was more interested in how he'd crossed the desert than just who he was or how he'd managed to get kilt. He didn't talk too much English. But a miner who'd once trapped beaver was able to get him to trace a few lines across an ordinance map. The dying Injun said there was two old trails marked out, once you rid northwest as far as Skull Mesa. He said one was good enough for cattle but that the other one was salty all the way.

"Well, then he died. A while later an army patrol showed up. They tried the cattle trail, the one running around the south side of Skull Mesa, and it worked, more or less. The old Siwash was mighty ignorant of cattle, but there's enough water along that route to keep men and mules alive, if they pack along enough canteens. We told them emigrants they were loco to attempt the trail with oxen in high summer, but you know how greenhorns are."

Longarm didn't answer. He knew human nature as well. An ox-drawn wagon moved slower than a child could walk, and so many a wagon master who should have known better had been tempted in the past, and would no doubt be tempted in the future, to save a few miles that made more sense on the map than when one got there. Had it been up to Longarm, there would have been a law against so called cutoff trails. The Walker cutoff had led one wagon train smack into Death Valley back in the gold rush days, and everyone knew what had happened to the Donner party when they decided the Hastings cutoff would save them a few days. Instead of raking up mistakes of the dead past, Longarm asked Culhane, "What about the *other* trail the old man mentioned? Has anyone ever tried it?"

Culhane shook his head. "Why should anyone? The trail the dumb old Injun said was fit for a cattle drive is bad enough. If there's one thing we don't need around here it's salt. Desert Injuns can take their drinking water more brackish than we can to begin with. So when an *Injun* says a line of water holes is salty, you'd best take his word for it!"

The thought inspired Culhane to some more beer. As he inhaled suds, Longarm glanced out the window again. "Well, it's too hot out for my mules and, to tell the truth, I prefer my riding a mite cooler. So I'd best hole up till sundown and ride after them wagons in the cool of evening. Meanwhile, I sure could use a map showing that Siwash Trail. And, if it ain't too much bother, you might point me at whatever you use for a hotel in this town while you're waiting for someone to build a proper one."

Culhane said, "There ain't no map of the Siwash Trail. The army stole the one the old Siwash drawed. But it's easy enough to follow, now. Like I said, it got traveled some during the Paiute troubles, and desert brush takes forever to grow back. You just ride out to the northwest, across the sage flats, till you see a mesa on the horizon. It's the only mesa there is out that way. I don't know why they calls it Skull Mesa. Anyways, there's a spring at the base of the mesa you can't miss, since it's almost choked with cottonwood and willow. From the water hole there's a beaten path aimed dead at

12

the mesa. Then she branches at a big old boulder. You follows the one running around to the south of the high ground. A day's ride on, there's another water hole. Only you'd best ride at night. And the water tastes like soap. You water your critters good, there, anyways. For from there on the trail takes you out across the Black Rock Desert, as it's so laughingly called. The wagon ruts beeline across the open playa a good thirty miles and, if there's any standing water, and you're fool enough to even taste it, you don't belong out here off a leash."

The old desert rat grimaced and said, "Lord, it makes me thirsty just *talking* about it." He took another swallow of beer before he continued. "The old Injun's trail takes you to the right gap in the Black Rock Range beyond, of course. Miss the passage through them bare black peaks and you'll soon learn how thirsty a man can get up a dry box canyon. Once you follows the trail through the Black Rock Range it's more desert, with three out of four water holes pure alkali, and not too many water holes of any description to worry on. Fort Bidwell's about sixty or seventy miles beyond the Black Rocks as the crow could make her. Takes longer on the ground, since the trail twists some to avoid jaggedy outcroppings, swamps filt with washing soda, and such. I warned them emigrants to for God's sake stick to the wagon ruts of them as went afore. I sure hope they paid attention. This time of the year there's mirage water tempting even sensible folk from every side, and there's no drinking water at *all* off the trail, no matter how much one might notice."

Longarm nodded. "Oxen move slower than mules, even at a walk. So I ought to catch up, riding at a trot at

13

night. But that still leaves me almost a full day to kill and I won't be able to ride worth mention if I spend the whole day sitting in this saloon."

Culhane nodded and said, "It's past my bedtime, too. I'd invite you home with me, but we only got one bed. You might try the Widow Westbury. Yellow house ahint the Western Union office. She takes in boarders now and again and she don't allow bedbugs. Tell her I sent you and she won't rob you too bad if she knows what's good for her."

Longarm rose, picked up his Winchester, and they shook hands. He left Culhane to finish another beer. As Longarm parted the batwing doors and stepped out on the plank walk, the sun was all the way up and everything more than a hundred yards off was shimmering in the oven-hot air. But the air was so thin and dry that the shade of the plank overhang shading the walk made an amazing difference. It was still too hot, but just bearable. Longarm headed for the telegraph office. He unbuttoned his shirt some more but left his frock coat on for now. It was a greenhorn trick to face the desert in rolled-up shirtsleeves.

He passed the office of the stage line, but he didn't go in to ask questions. He had already talked to the only man in town who might have known something important. He spotted the mustard-yellow frame house behind the more weatherbeaten shed of Western Union. He went on to the telegraph office first. The clerk on duty inside looked wilted, as he had every right to. Longarm helped himself to a yellow blank and a stub pencil on the counter. He blocked out a terse message to his boss, informing Vail that the fool colonel from Vienna had managed to get lost and asking permission to call it a day. He told the clerk to send it day rates. He knew Vail would want him to keep going, but it was worth a try.

The clerk complimented Longarm on his neat lettering and said he would have it on the wire long before anyone in Denver could have lunch. Longarm said, "Hold the thought a second, pard. I know you ain't allowed to divulge private messages of one client to another, but I ain't a client, I'm federal law. So I'm used to winning such arguments, with or without a court order."

The clerk looked too tired to argue. Longarm said, "Just tell me whether a tall foreigner with a dueling scar and a bitty waxed moustache sent a wire from here to anywhere, and we'll say no more about it."

The clerk looked blank, then brightened and said, "Say, there *was* such a gent in here. Let me see . . . night before last, it was. Is he wanted by the law, Deputy Long?"

Longarm sighed. "I wish he was. He's harder to catch up with than half the owlhoots I've gone after. No two men could look so funny. But just for the record, did he call himself Herr Oberst Von Thaldorf?"

The clerk frowned. "He might have. We don't keep records once a telegram's been accepted at the other end. I recalls him as a snooty ramrod-backed dude with a Dutch way of talking. That Von name rings a bell, too. He sent a wire to Washington. Damn my eyes if I recalls the exact address. He come in fast, writ fast, paid fast, and left the same way. Oh, yeah, he asked if there was somewhere around here a man could buy a mule in a hurry. I told him I was new in town. Don't know if he ever got his mule or not."

Longarm nodded and said, "Since he ain't here, he

must have. Do you remember whether he was here before or after that emigrant train passed through?"

The clerk shrugged. "I don't pay much attention to the front window when I'm busy. It was the same night, now that I think back. Does it really matter?"

Longarm shook his head and said he would come by later to see if there was any reply to his own wire. Then he stepped outside.

He was about to circle to the Widow Westbury's when he heard the distant rumble of steel-shod hooves and wheels. He turned to watch. A distant shimmering dot came in off the desert and turned into a Concord coach and six-mule team. He doubted anyone he was expecting could be arriving from Rye Patch after him, but life was filled with surprises. So he stood in the shade, Winchester cradled over one arm, to wait and see.

The coach had obviously started while it was still dark and been caught out on the flats by the rising sun. From the way its crew was driving the lathered mules, they must have wanted some beer, too. The coach lumbered past and braked to a swaying stop in front of the line's office just down the way. A skinny dishwater blonde in a faded print dress came out of the office to fuss at them for abusing company property so. The driver cussed her back and got down to unload the boot as the shotgun messenger helped the passengers out.

The first one out was a red-headed woman with a handsome figure. Longarm could tell, even though her tan travel duster was loosely cut, by the way it clung to her curves. She headed into the station, nose in the air and walking fast.

The only other passenger to alight was a gent in a

16

derby hat and checked summer suit. He was pale-faced, even for a dude, and stood near the coach, looking about sort of shifty, as if he had something on his conscience.

He did. Longarm was good at remembering faces, so shaving off the beard and dressing like a dude hadn't worked after all. Longarm levered a round into the chamber of his Winchester, but stayed put in the shade as he called out, "Morning, Spuds. I surely hope you can see just how dumb it would be to resist arrest at this range with that hogleg under your coat."

Spuds Taylor, late of Leavenworth Prison, must not have. He went for the Patterson Conversion riding his right hip. Longarm snorted in disgust and fired the Winchester he had already trained on the desperate fool.

The .44-40 slug shoved the owlhoot back against a big rear wheel of the coach. The wheel spokes were dusty yellow when he slammed into them. He painted a dotted line of ruby red on them as he slid down to his knees but, by some stubborn effort of will, slowly drew his old thumbuster. Longarm called out, "Give it up, Spuds. It's too hot a day to get shot twice."

Taylor stared his way, slack-jawed, then sobbed and tossed his own gun out of reach in the alkali dust. Longarm nodded and moved over to join the man he had just gunned. The coach crew had moved around to the far side, out of sight as well as out of the line of fire. Longarm called out to them, "Lest you gents make an awful mistake, I'm law, and this gent praying against your coach wheel ain't. I sure wish I had some help moving him into the shade."

The man at his feet sobbed, "Don't touch me, damn

17

your eyes! Can't you see I'm too mortal wounded to move?"

"You do look a might green around the gills, Spuds. Where did I hull you and how bad?"

"I ain't sure. It feels like a bad case of heartburn indeed, and if you had any decent feelings you'd finish me afore the shock wears off, Longarm."

"You know I ain't allowed to do that, Spuds. But you'd best let us move you into the shade, at least. It's hot as hell out here in the sunlight. Must be a hundred in the shade, but that's still an improvement."

The gutshot owlhoot muttered, "Do tell? It don't feel hot to me. Matter of fact, I feels sort of *cold* right now. It don't hurt as bad where you hit me, neither. How in God's name did you catch up with me, you sneaky rascal? I was sure I was in the clear, once I got past the Rockies. There was nothing about our jail break in the Salt Lake papers."

By now both the dishwater blonde and the redhead were staring their way from the station steps. Old Culhane and a younger deputy were coming down the street faster than the heat and dust really called for. As they joined him, Longarm said, "This here is the late Spuds Taylor. He was doing twenty to life at Leavenworth for an earlier misunderstanding we had regarding a federal payroll job. As you can see, he didn't fancy staying there. As I hope you know, there's a standing federal bounty on army deserters and escaped federal prisoners, if you follow my drift."

Culhane did. "It's sure a good thing I recognized him so good. We got a deal on the paperwork, old son. But hadn't we best carry him into the shade to die more comfortable?"

Longarm said, "We already discussed that. As you can see from the way he's turning yellow under his prison pallor, he's bleeding inside with considerable enthusiasm. So just be patient."

He hunkered down by the dying man to add, not unkindly, "If you have anyone you want us to get in touch with, Spuds, you'd best spit it out while you still can."

Taylor told him to go to hell, then asked, "No shit, Longarm, how did you cut me off so slick? I know your rep, and I'll allow you lived up to it the *last* time you caught up with me, but this is *ridiculous!*"

Longarm shot a warning glance up at his fellow lawmen to button their lips as he lied, sincerely, "I reckon it won't hurt to tell you true, Spuds. You was peached on by the pals you was on your way to join."

Spuds Taylor shook his head as if to clear it and growled, "That can't be, Longarm. You're trying to slicker me, ain't you?"

"Suit yourself. I reckon it's best if you just wait for 'em in hell, secure in the belief they had no use for the bounty on such hot merchandise, Spuds. Having spent more time behind bars than us, you likely know how trustworthy your breed is."

The dying man sobbed, "It ain't fair! I was supposed to meet *kin* out here, God damn everyone entire!"

Then he fell forward to lie face down in the dust. Longarm put a hand to the side of his neck and insisted, "Where was you to meet your kin, Spuds? Here in town or out on the Siwash Trail?"

Taylor coughed and gasped, "Water hole, out where there ain't no law, and . . ." Then he was dead.

Longarm got back to his feet. Culhane said, "That

was pretty slick, Longarm. You got him to admit he was headed up the Siwash Trail to meet someone!"

Longarm sighed. "Yeah, only all we know now is that they're blood kin to a man I just gunned, and that they're waiting somewhere betwixt here and Fort Bidwell. After that, they could be just about anyone I meet on the trail. I'm sure looking forward to heading out alone across the desert after dark. But first I mean to get out of this infernal sun."

Chapter 2

The Widow Westbury was a pleasant surprise. She was a buxom brunette of around thirty, who, lest anyone mistake her ample proportions for pure lard, kept the sash of her pongee kimono clinched tight around a twenty-four inch waist. Had the pale pongee been any thinner he would have been able to count individual hairs under it. As it was, it was only easy to establish that she was brunette all over and had a mole over her left nipple. She said he could call her Babs and that she'd be proud to hire him a room for the day.

As she led him back through darker surroundings she said over her shoulder, "I wasn't expecting gentlemen callers, as you can see. But one must be practical about attire once it gets this hot, don't you agree?"

He said he'd met Indian ladies dressed more practical and that as soon as he could he meant to shuck entirely. Babs Westbury laughed and said, "Not so loud. The neighbors might hear. Here's the room I have to let. The bath is just next door here. Indoor plumbing is not a luxury out here, it's a dire necessity, winter or summer."

Longarm asked if by any chance she had an indoor bath. She said, "I can do better than that. I have a stall shower. The nozzle came all the way from Paris, France, where folk know how to live decent. I surely admire French ways, don't you?"

He didn't know how to answer that. The trouble with women who talked forward was that a man still couldn't tell. He was more in need of a cool shower and a stretch-out atop clean sheets than he was a slap in the head. He followed her into the small but clean-looking bedroom without further discussion. The shades were drawn, of course, but it was still too sunny all over Rosebud Wash this time of day. Babs hesitated in the doorway until he nodded in satisfaction. Then she said, "I usually get four bits a day and I notice you brought no luggage, save for that rifle."

Longarm leaned the Winchester in a corner and got out two quarters. He explained that he'd left his saddles and such at the livery. She looked relieved as he paid in advance, and asked if there was anything else she could do for him.

He shook his head. "No, thanks. I won't even need a towel. For I meant to cool off in the shower next door and lie down wet, if you don't mind."

She told him to go ahead, as she always changed the

linen between boarders in any case. He wondered why she didn't go away so he could strip. Since it was her house, there was no polite way to ask her to. She waited out the awkward silence for a time. Then she said, "Well, I'd best get out of this hot outfit in my own little bed. Try to make a little noise as you wander about back here naked. For I mean to take at least three showers myself, today, and it wouldn't do for us to bump into one another in a state of pure nature, would it?"

Longarm agreed the notion sounded scandalous and she left. He waited until he was alone in there. Then he got out of his duds, hung everything up, and cracked the door to make sure the coast was clear. He saw that it was and ducked next door, closing the door behind him and hanging his gun rig on it. He inspected his surroundings in the gloom. There was no tub, but there was a handsome sink and, sure enough, a stall shower built into a corner with an oilcloth curtain to keep the cork floor tiles reasonably dry. He parted the curtain and stepped in to try the hot water tap. He wasn't surprised when the water came out cold. It was still warmer than Denver tap water, since the pipes of Rosebud Wash no doubt ran shallow from wherever the town drew its water. He stepped under the cascade and sighed with pure pleasure. He hadn't known he was so overheated until he got to cool off some. There was a sliver of pink soap in a wire holder above the taps. He lathered himself good, hair and all, and even though he had known he hadn't had a decent bath since Denver, he was still surprised at how much crud went running down the drain between his bare feet. He put the soap back and let the running water rinse him clean. He didn't want to get out, ever. Now that he was used to the first cooling shock, the water felt just right. He knew that no matter how long he stayed under it, he would no doubt feel hot again less than an hour after he hit the sack.

But he did have a long, hard night ride ahead of him, and he hadn't slept the night before. He decided he'd best bite the bullet and was about to shut off the tap and get out when the curtain suddenly parted and his land-lady gasped, "Oh, you startled me!"

That made two of them, since the big brunette was as naked as he was and seemed to be climbing in there with him instead of screaming off down the corridor the way a lady was supposed to on such occasions.

He moved back to make room for her. He had few other choices, since she had him boxed and hadn't in-vited him to bump asses with her yet.

She got under the water, grabbed the soap, and got right down to business with it, all over, as she demurely explained, "I thought by now you'd have finished in here. But seeing as the damage has been done, and see-ing it's too dark to really see too much—"

"I ain't complaining," he cut in, reaching out to take her soap-slicked body in his own wet arms.

She flinched away and turned her back to him. "Sir! What kind of a woman do you take me for?" she pro-tested.

"A gal who takes showers with a man?" he tried.

She just kept her back to him and insisted, "I'm sim-ply trying to save water. So don't get the wrong idea about my pragmatic approach to survival in desert coun-try."

He was trying not to. But she had him backed against the wet wall with her soapy behind and he was begin-ning to rise to the occasion despite his efforts not to. If it rose any further, she'd feel it for sure, and they both knew his real gun was hanging on the door outside. She said, "Oh, God, the only time I feel human after the Fourth of July is under this shower. I'm sorry I burst in on you like this. But as long as you're here, would you mind soaping my back? It's a luxury I've missed since my late husband fell down a mine shaft a year ago."

He took the soap and got to work with it. He suspected from the way she crooned with pleasure that getting her back soaped wasn't the only creature comfort she'd been missing lately. It was all he could do to keep from soaping her more private parts as well. It was giving him a raging erection, despite the cool water running down between them. He said, "I've soaped you everywhere a gent ought to, ma'am. You'd best take back the bar before we get in trouble."

She laughed, reached blindly for the soap, and dropped it. "Oh, damn," she said, and bent over to pick it up, thrusting back further with her slippery, naked rump. What happened then was hardly as surprising as she seemed to take it. She gasped, "Oh, what do you think you're *doing*, sir?" as Longarm cupped a hip bone in either hand and hauled her on all the way, saying, "Offering you more luxury, ma'am. Grab your own ankles and it'll feel even better."

She protested, "You're *raping* me, you brute!" even as she bent down to grasp his rather than her ankles to take it even deeper. He didn't argue. Some gals felt comforted by the notion it wasn't their own fault, and it hardly mattered what she *said* as long as she kept *moving* like that.

She did, as the water ran down her spine to stream off her long black hair. The contrast between the cool

25

shower and her warm pulsating interior was delightful to Longarm. She moaned and told him, "Oh, let's finish *right* in *bed,* darling!"

So he picked her up and carried her next door to do as she requested. He was coming in her a third time when Babs giggled and said, "This is amazing. Do you realize we've never even kissed yet?"

He said that was no problem and kissed her good as they came hard together. Then he said, "What say you give a man a chance to catch his second wind so's we can make a day instead of a contest out of it?"

Babs snuggled closer and allowed she was a mite winded, too, but added, "Just so you don't plan on leaving me still hot once it cools off, you rascal. Do you really have to leave at sundown? I mean, I wouldn't charge, did you want to stay over a day or so."

He chuckled fondly and replied, "I'd admire that a heap, honey. But I wasn't sent all the way out here to tickle you fancy, no offense." Then, lest she feel hurt, he quickly added, "I might be coming back this way once I find out why I've come so far."

That seemed to cheer her, but of course it meant he had to tell her what he was doing out here in the first place. He brought her up to date on his case in as few words as possible, since it hardly seemed important. But when he got to the part about the old Indian, Babs chimed in, "Oh, I remember *him*. I was one of the ladies as spoon-fed him chicken broth as he lay dying in the back room at the Silver Spur. The poor old Siwash was grateful, I could tell, even though he couldn't talk American."

Longarm frowned thoughtfully and asked, "If he

couldn't savvy our lingo word one, who told you he was a Siwash, and how did he map out the Siwash Trail?"

"Oh, that's easy. A mountain man called Clown O'Shay was working here in town at the time. He'd learned lots of Indian words in his day, and of course he spoke Sign as well. So they worked things out betwixt 'em. Clown was the one as figured him for a Siwash. The rest of us had him down as a Digger. For he rid in bare-ass as well as bare-back on a steel-shod pony Clown said he'd likely stolen."

Longarm said, "That mountain man was cussing him, not naming him, if he called him a Siwash. Could you say where Clown O'Shay might be these days?"

She draped a lush thigh across him and proceeded to toy with the hair on his chest as she replied with a yawn, "Clown's dead. He got in a drunken brawl a few months after the old Indian died, and wound up the same way. My late husband said Clown had a drinking problem, though he was always a gent around me. If you ain't up to screwing some more, would you mind if I dozed a spell, darling? I must say there's nothing like a cold shower and a warm screwing to relax a body."

He waited till she was snoring softly on his bare shoulder. Then he eased her off before she could sweat him up more.

She sighed and rolled on her belly. He moved to a cooler stretch of bedding and closed his eyes. He knew they would both wind up too hot to sleep before noon. He faced some serious riding, and two nights in a row without sleep could be pushing it. So he told himself to join Babs in the arms of Morpheus. But though his body was tired enough, his brain was still running in circles.

27

He kept trying to talk trade Chinook in his own sleepy head. It was more a made-up baby talk, like pidgin English, than a real language. Less than half the Indians talking it, and naturally none of the whites, were really Chinook. It was a mishmash of Indian, English, and French-Canadian words strung together.

He told himself not to bother, since it seemed hardly likely he would ever get to talk to either the dead Indian or the dead mountain man, and the two of them had obviously worked things out well enough. For there would have been no Siwash Trail if the old man called a Siwash had not been able to communicate at all. But, in that case, why had the mountain man cursed him as a worthless trash Indian, which was what Siwash meant when one got down to cases?

Longarm muttered aloud, "Hell, the Indian was likely cursing, too, as he lay dying full of chicken soup, and the white man was a drunk who liked to get in fights. It's as easy to fathom the mind of a woman as it is a mean drunk, and no man with a lick of sense has ever been able to fathom either one!"

The buxom woman at his side proved his point an hour or so later when, just as he was snoring regular, she woke him up again, hot and bothered both ways.

Chapter 3

It always took a while for the desert to cool off after sundown. So Longarm gave old Babs a friendly farewell and she gave him coffee and homemade chocolate cake to remember her by. Her screwing was a lot better than her cooking, but he put away three cups of strong black coffee to clear his head.

Then he kissed her goodbye and headed for the Western Union around the corner. Inside, he found that Billy Vail had answered his wire and wanted him to keep trying to catch up with that Austro–Hungarian lawman. Washington had him listed as missing in the Great American Desert and wanted him found before the Emperor Franz Josef noticed.

Vail's wire added:

I TOLD THEM NOT TO BE SILLY ABOUT LOCAL DIGGERS STOP BUT STATE ALERT- ED FORT BIDWELL ANYWAY STOP BE CAREFUL STOP YOU KNOW HOW TRIGGER HAPPY THE ARMY CAN GET STOP VAIL US MARSHAL DENVER DISTRICT COURT.

Longarm sent back a night letter, saying he would ride at least as far as Fort Bidwell before he begged to come home again. Then he went to the livery and helped the Mexican saddle the two mules for him. He put the pack saddle on the mule he had ridden the night before.

As he settled accounts with old Greaser Bill, the liveryman said, "Oh, I almost forgot. There was a lady asking for you here a couple of hours ago. I told her you were not here."

Longarm frowned. "That was truthful enough, I reckon. Did she leave a name or, better yet, say what she wanted with my fair white body?"

Greaser Bill smirked. "*She* was the one with the body. If she left a name, I forget it. She was a most handsome redhead, who spoke English worse than myself. She did not say for why she wanted you. But one could see she wanted you most urgently. I think she said she was staying at the stage station. They hire a couple of rooms upstairs, for people with business here in Rosebud Wash."

Longarm grinned. "I'm glad Bull Culhane never told me so. Hang on to these critters and . . . Never mind, I'll lead 'em over and let 'em get used to the night air while I have a jaw with the redhead."

He tethered the mules out front and went inside. The same washed-out little blonde was on duty behind the ticket counter. He ticked his hatbrim at her and told her what he was doing there. She nodded but said, "Frostline Osterhoff just checked out, sir."

Longarm frowned thoughtfully and asked, "Are you sure that first part wasn't *Fraulein,* ma'am?"

The dishwater blonde shrugged. "Sounded like Frostline to me. She talked funny. Said she was an Australian lady. I never got her whole story. I wasn't interested."

"It was a mighty warm day where *I* was, too. Could you try an educated guess as to what an Austrian fraulein might want with me, ma'am?"

The blonde nodded. "That's easy. After you shot that cuss out front this morning we both naturally thought to ask how come. She got all excited when the townees said you was the one and only Longarm. But by that time you was gone. She couldn't find you. Where did you go, by the way? I sent her to all the places an honest stranger could wind up in this one-horse town, but you wasn't in any of 'em."

He said, "I cannot tell a lie. I was in church all afternoon. Did she say where she was heading when she checked out?"

The blonde shook her head. "I didn't ask, and she didn't say. She had a round trip out of Rye Patch, though. Might have gone back on the sundown stage. I was out back as they was loading up. I hope she ain't wanted by the law."

He shrugged and said, "The law didn't know she was

31

in the country till just now. If she ever comes back, still looking for me, tell her I ain't here no more. The next place I can be reached by wire or any other way will be Fort Bidwell, over in the Alkali Lake country."

"You ain't taking the Siwash Trail, in high summer?"

"You know another way to get to Fort Bidwell, ma'am?"

"Sure I do. You take the train at Rye Patch all the way out to California. Then you follows the Applegate or some other sensible trail north to the army wagon trace. I told some fool emigrants the same thing the other night, but would they listen?"

He sighed. "They likely figured on saving a few hundred miles of freight charges. I'd best be going if I mean to catch up with their party."

"You will, well this side of Fort Bidwell. For our company surveyed the Siwash Trail years ago, with a view to saving them same miles."

"And?"

"And it's best to go the long way 'round. A stage line needs a line of stages, and such water and grass as there might be out there is too far apart. They pay us extra for manning this awful station. There ain't enough money on earth to hire a station crew stuck out on the even worse flats of the Black Rock."

"But your survey crew did get back all right?"

"Sure. They took plenty of canteens and they knew what they were doing. But they swore they'd never do it again. The Siwash Trail was never intended for wheeled vehicles, Deputy Long. It's hard enough on riders traveling light. Ask the post office if you don't believe me."

He nodded absently. Then he frowned and said, "Run

that part by me again. Are you saying Uncle Sam sends *mail* along the Siwash Trail?"

"Not exactly. Private contractors carry mail pouches from Rye Patch to that army post now and again. We was interested in the contract till we found the route was so rough. A couple of brothers called Bradford bid on it and got it. They live in Rye Patch and they take turns running mail along the trail as need be. I got their address somewhere if you really want it."

He reached in his coat for his notebook. Then he shook his head and said, "Don't bother, ma'am. I got enough on my plate to worry me. If I meet up with what looks like a leftover pony express rider out there, I'll know who he is. If I don't, it won't matter."

He thanked her for her encouraging words about the trail and left to see if she really knew what she was talking about.

By midnight he was beginning to suspect she did. The desert air was cool enough to make him glad he was wearing tweed, although the sun-baked sage all around was still giving off heat. The moon was high. The sky, of course, was so clear a man could no doubt reach up and pluck some stars, if he really stretched. But Culhane had said Skull Mesa was out here somewhere, and though Longarm could see for miles across the moonlit sage, he didn't see a bump high enough to matter, and he had to be a good twenty miles out of town by now.

It got worse around three in the morning. The wind started blowing. It was a cold, dry wind out of the west. The dust it kicked up was sand-blasting his left cheek above the kerchief he tied over his mouth. Wetting the red calico helped, but some dust still got through, and

33

his mouth began to taste like a mummy's armpit. He knew the mules were suffering, too, even though they couldn't say so. He called out, "We'll shelter from this infernal wind as soon as we come to some shelter, pards."

But there wasn't anything higher than a sagebrush no matter which way he looked. So he reined in, dismounted, and swung both mules' rumps to the wind. It didn't help as much as he had hoped. The dust was fine as a woman's face powder and tasted just as awful. He tried hunkering down, but it was worse closer to the ground. He swore and decided, "Well, I'd just as soon be *going* somewhere while I get run over by a dust dune, and there's water and trees somewhere ahead, pards."

He remounted and forged on. The moon still shone and the sky was too clear to be real. But now everything at ground level was hidden under a ghostly white haze. The pack mule was starting to fight the lead rope now. He swore at it and said, "I know where we're going, as long as I can still see the stars, damn it. I know it's a good idea to turn back, but we can't, so cut that out."

His eyes were full of dust and breathing was getting to be a real problem. Then, as suddenly as it had whipped up, the wind died.

He wiped his eyes with the corner of the kerchief and by the time he could see again the dust had settled and, better yet, a low tabletopped rise lay ahead in the moonlight, only a mile or so farther to his left than he'd been aiming. He laughed and told his mount, "That has to be the mesa Culhane mentioned. It's a good thing the wind died in time, for damned if we wasn't headed for that

34

salty trail the old Indian warned about. Let's see if we can find that water."

They did. Trees gleaming silver in the moonlight were easy to spot from a distance. The mules both tried to bolt as they smelled water. He held them to the same pace, warning them that was no way to travel in desert country. But he let them run the last quarter of a mile. By then he was finding dry sage tedious company, as well.

The spring was a tiny paradise after the long night ride, even though in truth it was just a clump of dusty cottonwoods and weeds around a muddy puddle. Longarm let the mules drink, since Culhane had said the water was safe. He refreshed himself with canteen water and held off refilling for now. The water would be even safer once the dust the wind had just blown into it had a chance to settle.

He glanced up at the sky and announced, "We made better time, this far, than ox-drawn wagons could have. It's fixing to lighten up in an hour or so. If we go on, the sun figures to catch us out in open desert again. So I vote we hole up here, where there's shade as well as water. What do you boys say to that?"

Neither mule answered. Longarm removed both saddles and tethered them on long leads so they could graze and water as they willed. He unlashed his bedroll and dragged it into the thickest clump of woods he could find, northwest of the water. As he unrolled it on the dry grass and leaf litter he spied a sardine can glinting in the moonlight. He picked it up and gave it a sniff before casting it away. He grimaced and said aloud, "Opened and eaten within a few days. Salty canned fish sure was dumb for desert rations."

35

He wondered where the wagon train would be making camp about now as he propped his Winchester in a tree crotch, hung his sidearm as handy near the head of the bedroll, and proceeded to undress.

He knew he had eaten up some of their lead by now. But since they had such a good one on him, it hardly seemed likely he could catch up in less than forty-eight hours. On the other hand, there was no place else the fool colonel could be for the next full week or so.

He lay naked under the stars atop his blankets, resisting the temptation to cover up as the cool desert air goose-bumped him. He knew once the sun was up he would be frying even in the shade. He aimed to soak up as much coolness as he could before sunrise.

But he was too keyed up to sleep, and after a time he felt so cold he just had to give in. He pulled a blanket over himself, muttering, "Ain't life a bitch? Nothing's ever just right. When it's cold you want it hot, and when it's hot you can't remember ever being cold."

He reached for his nearby shirt and fished out a smoke and a match. He thumbed alight, lit his cheroot, and stared up at the sky as the Milky Way began to give way to the deep purple of a desert dawn. Then he heard hoofbeats coming his way fast and forgot his recent plans to sleep late that morning.

He sat up, hauled on his pants, and strapped his gun on before he even considered his boots. So he was standing barefoot, naked from the waist up, when the mystery rider burst through the brush and splashed stirrup-deep into the water hole. Longarm called out, "For God's sake, that's no way to treat *water* out here, you asshole!"

Then he got a better look at the rider. "Oops, sorry, ma'am. I thought you was the U. S. Mail."

The girl sitting sidesaddle on a black stud too big for her to handle called back, "I tried to hold him back when he smelled water but—*Ach, Gott,* such a stubborn he ist!"

Then she asked, "Are you Herr Longarm? I have for you all over been searching."

He said, "You found me, Fraulein Osterhoff . . . if that's your name."

She said it was and tried to haul her mount's head up out of the water so she could alight dry-shod. Longarm waded in, grabbed her mount's bridle, and gave the bit a good yank to reset it. "That's enough water for anyone but a camel, horse. Where did you get this ridiculous critter, fraulein?"

She replied, "From the livery, when der Mexicaner told me you had left about an hour before. I thought a mistake I had made when that dust began to blow out there. Had not this horse water smelt, I fear I was lost. Where are we *now?* Do you know?"

He said, "I do, and you're still lost, aboard that water hog you hired."

He led them both out of the roiled pool and helped her dismount. "It's suicide for you to go on and too late for you to head back, now that the sun's about up," he told her. "I'll tether this brute for you. Meanwhile, you'll find a bedroll over yonder to sit down on. If you'd rather squat, after such a long ride, go down the other way, amidst that willow brush, downwind."

She gasped. "Ist that any way to speak to a lady, *mein herr?*"

"Out here the facts of life are more important than tea-party manners, ma'am. I was being polite, in my own country way. If you insist you ain't built like the rest of the human race, I won't offer no more well-meant advice on camping out."

As he finished, her over-watered mount began to piss up a storm. She laughed despite herself as he led it away from the water hole, lest it foul their only drinking water. Then she lit out as he unsaddled her mount, rubbed its back dry with the saddle blanket, and found a stout tree to hold it for a spell. "I know you're dumber than any mule, horse. But if you run off when the heat and flies start to fret you, you'll never make her back to town before the sun drops you."

He found the Austrian redhead seated demurely on his bedroll. He sat down beside her, snuffing out his cheroot, and said, "They told me back in town you was looking for me. You want to tell me why, Fraulein?"

She dimpled at him in the rosy dawn light. "You may call me Herta, since I hope we can be friends. Ist so, you are a famous Wild-Wester sheriff, und that you haf been asked to help das terrible Oberst Von Thaldorf for our Hansel to search?"

He smiled sheepishly. "I'm a Deputy U. S. Marshal not a sheriff, and lots of other things folk say about me are fibs, too. I have been ordered to assist your colonel from Vienna town. Is Hansel another way of referring to one Hans Krinke, wanted for counterfeiting, jailbreak, and Lord knows what-all?"

She almost sobbed. "Hansel ist not a criminal. He was not bank notes printing as they say. They were political exposés, written by Crown Prince Rudolf himself! You see, Prince Rudolf ist not like other Hapsburgs. He ist a true liberal und a friend of the people. Even if he was not, how can *Hansel* be blamed for what his own prince wrote und ordered him to publish?"

Longarm sighed and said, "That's easy, when one ain't a prince. But your story don't make much sense, no offense. I got it on good authority your Hans Krinke asked for political asylum and got turned down. If what you say is halfway true, how come? Washington allowed old Juarez to live in Texas, writing awful things about the Emperor of Mexico, and now that I study on it, old Max was a Hapsburg, too."

She placed a cool hand on his bare forearm as she leaned closer and almost whispered, "They charged Hans Krinke with counterfeiting, not subversive publishing, for that very reason. They had to put a stop to what Prince Rudolf was doing and, naturally, they could not a crown prince arrest, you see?"

"That makes a mite more sense. Ain't sure that *prince* does, though. For if he's the crown prince, don't that mean he gets to be the emperor some sunnier day?"

She nodded but explained, "Franz Josef is only middle of age as well as iron of fist. Prince Rudolf is young und idealistic. He fears that by the time he could become emperor, there might *be* no Austro–Hungarian Empire. Too close with Imperial Prussia has the court become, so our own as well as the Magyar suffer under der same zoke, und . . ."

"Back up," Longarm said with a frown. "What in thunder is a Magyar?"

She said, "*Ach*, I forget the English for Magyar ist Hungarian. You see, the Hapsburg Empire is a patchwork of many races, held in das iron fist of one crazy

39

German-speaking family. Prince Rudolf feels even the iron fist must fail in the end. So he wishes to propose ein constitution granting more justice, und less iron fist. All poor Hansel Krinke did was print und distribute das proposal for Prince Rudolf. Der prince has very sound ideas for a boy of seventeen, you see, so . . ."

"Oh, Lord," Longarm said. "We're talking about a teenager talking back to his elders? It's small wonder old Franz Josef had a fit. My old man would have switched me good had I argued with *him* at seventeen, and I hardly ever proposed overthrowing the statutes of West-by-God-Virginia. But let's see if I get this straight. Before I take your word on false charges, just where do you and this Krinke jasper dovetail together?"

She looked blank.

"If that was too country, try her this way. Are you kin to Hans Krinke, married up with him, or what?" he asked.

She said, "Oh, I am not so close as *that* to him. He was with mein brother a classmate at the university, und of course we are all of the same political party."

"What party might that be?"

"We are working for the socialist movement of Karl Marx."

He whistled softly and said, "I wonder why they only charged Krinke with counterfeiting. It's as easy to hang murder one on an avowed Marxist, and they do, lots of places this side of Vienna town. I see why old Franz Josef is so sore, now. The Vanderbilts ain't half as royal and *they'd* likely have a fit if a moody teenager got to writing Marxist broadsides when he was supposed to be doing his homework."

She pouted. "Are you not a working man, Herr Long?" she demanded.

"Call me Custis, and I sure am," he said. "I've been trying all my life to figure out a way to get by *without* working, but so far I ain't had much luck. Before you recite the *Communist Manifesto* to me, Herta, I already read it, and, no offense, it's pure twaddle."

"How can you say that? Don't you feel oppressed? Can you not see you have all your life been exploited by the idle rich?"

He nodded. "Sure I can. I herded cows before I got this better job with Justice. Anyone with the brains of a gnat can see life ain't fair. Most of us get born, enjoy a little fun and a lot of tedium, and then we die. Fate deals some of us better hands than others, even though nobody beats the house in the end. But old Marx misses the point entire. He seems to think fate gives us all a choice before we're born. If that was true, I'll be switched if I can see why anyone would choose in advance to be born to poor and ignorant parents instead of bloated plutocrats. It ain't my fault I'm who I is. So I got to accord them Vanderbilts the same courtesy. If I cursed them for being born richer, I'd feel honor bound to tell poor colored folk I was sorry as hell I was white and making better than a dollar a day, wouldn't I?"

She smiled wryly. "I see you are a stubborn man as well as a capitalist tool. Let us not argue politics. Let us talk about poor Hansel Krinke und the terrible trouble he is in. You know, of course, der Oberst Von Thaldorf does not mean to take him alive?"

Longarm said, "This is the first I've heard of that notion. If I'm with the colonel when we catch up with

41

Krinke, and Krinke's willing to come quiet, there won't be no killing. I don't know what Prince Rudolf's constitution has to say on that point, but I know what our own does."

His words failed to comfort her. She insisted, "Even if Hansel ist alive taken, der Oberst will murder him as soon as he can, on the way back to Europe. You must not let him do this, Custis. Whether you agree with our political philosophy or not, Hansel Krinke does not deserve to die."

He shrugged his bare shoulders. "I won't argue that point. Queen Victoria allowed Karl Marx the freedom of London Town even as he was writing awful things about her kind. Hell, *we* have to be as democratic as the British! But you see, Herta, I have no say in the matter. I ain't under orders to arrest Hans Krinke. My orders are to tag along with Colonel Von Thaldorf and make sure nobody messes with *him.*"

The sun was peeping over the horizon now, and he could see a tear shining on her pretty cheek. He patted her hand. "Look, at the rate he's going, he might not catch Krinke at all. I don't even know what the cuss looks like, and if the colonel can't find him I ain't bound to."

She said, "Der Oberst ist a determined manhunter, und Hansel ist such a small und harmless man. They told me in Rosebud Wash that they thought Hansel was mitt das wagon train, and by now—"

"He ain't. He can't be," Longarm cut in.

She asked how he knew, and he told her, "The colonel rode out well ahead of me aboard another mule. I'll take your word he's set in his ways. So by now he must have caught up with the wagon train. If Hans Krinke

42

was with it, by now the colonel would have arrested him, stuffed him, or whatever, right?"

"Das ist all too true. He has standing orders to shoot Hansel on sight. But what if he already *has?*"

"I'm going out of my way for nothing," he replied. "I figure the colonel would have caught up with the wagons right about here. Surely no farther out than the next water hole, this side of the Black Rock. So where is the colonel if he got his man? He'd have no reason to go on to Fort Bidwell with the wagons if his deed was done, would he?"

She brightened. "Ach, Gott, das means Hansel must still be *ahead* of das wagon train, *nicht wahr?*"

"That's the way I reads such sign as there is, so far," he said. "Nobody actually saw Krinke join the wagon train. They just knew he must have left Rosebud Wash the same night. If he was riding alone, on the prod and knowing the law was close behind, he'd have gone twice as far by sunrise as any fool wagon could have."

She nodded thoughtfully, but being a woman she had to worry, so she asked, "What if Hansel ist in das desert lost? He ist a middle-class businessman, not a cowboy, *ja?*"

Longarm grimaced. "By now the thought should have crossed his mind. But it works the same way. If he wasn't still going, by now the colonel would have found him where he dropped."

"But der Oberst with the slower wagons ist, und das desert so wide ist, Custis."

He lay back on one elbow and plucked a grass stem to chew. "You can only chew the apple a bite at a time, Herta. We don't know for sure the colonel's still with them wagons. He might have found them too slow for his digestion and forged on ahead. He might be more sensible than anyone's said he is, so far. In that case he'll be with the wagons when I catch up, and Krinke won't. If Krinke don't show up under a cloud of buzzards this side of Fort Bidwell, it will mean he made it. After that, it's a whole new ball game, and I'd be a fool to offer any suggestions on the final score."

She insisted he try, anyway, so he said, "Fort Bidwell and beyond is still desert country, but it's more sensible desert country, which is why the army forted there to keep an eye on the Modoc after old Captain Jack went crazy a spell back. There's water holes, and even townships, west to where one can follow the old Applegate Trail north to the apple country of Oregon. The trail's named after two brothers called Applegate, not real apples, by the way. That part's just an accident. But I must say the Applegate's well named. Takes you smack into country where you have to step back quick when you toss aside an apple core, lest you get a tree up your —ah, never mind. The gent who explained it to me did so when no ladies was present."

"Und if Hansel reaches this Applegate without being murdered by Franz Josef's officer und executioner?" she asked.

He said, "Depends on who's telling the truth, most likely. There's lots of foreigners emigrating to the Northwest these days, and a man of any description don't stand out much in tall timber. If Krinke makes it to the settled parts of Oregon and keeps his nose clean, I doubt anyone will *ever* catch him. If he gets to printing funny money, he'll be in a hell of a mess. Them Oregonians don't trust paper money even when it's real, and it ain't safe to cheat a man who works all day with an *axe* in his hands."

She insisted her Hansel was no criminal and asked how soon they would be going on to see what they could do about the colonel who seemed to think he was. Longarm said, "I'm pushing on at sundown. You ain't. I already noticed you lit out without one infernal canteen lashed to that sissy saddle. So I'll treat you to one of mine, we'll water that stud good, and head you back to Rosebud Wash on your own."

She insisted that she wanted to go on with him.

"Look, we ain't arguing the point, Herta," he said. "It's a simple law of nature that you'd never make Fort Bidwell on that stable horse, even if I was dumb enough to let you try. You're already too far out to make her back by broad day. So simmer down, try to stay cool and rested, in such shade as there might be, and we'll say no more about it."

She agreed that it was getting warm for so early in the morning, so she unbuttoned her travel duster. She was wearing a blouse and a heavy velvet skirt under it. She unpinned her prissy little hat, shucked the poplin duster, and tossed it as far as she could, aiming at a bush. Her aim was tolerable, but as the duster draped over the clump it buzzed back at her.

She asked, "Wass ist das, ein hopper grasser?"

Longarm had to laugh. "Sounds more like a rattler to me," he said.

She blanched and demanded, "Ein rattler *snake,* you mean? *Ach, Gott!* What do you intend to *do* about it?"

He frowned up at her and asked, "Do what? Anyone can see that bush is a good ten feet away."

"*Ja,* but *under* it ist ein *rattler snake,* Custis!"

45

"So what? It can't hurt your duster, even did it aim to."

"Never mind mein duster! What about *us?*"

He smiled. "You're too big for a snake to eat, no offense. Desert rattlers never go for anything bigger than a rabbit. It's just seeking shade, like us. You startled it with your duster, so it buzzed to let your duster know it was there. It never meant no harm."

She shook her red curls and insisted, "You have to kill it. I am afraid it might bite me."

"Get on the other side of me, if you're scared," he said. "That old snake knows we're bigger than it, as well as *here*. Most snakebites is pure misunderstandings. That poor overheated rattler has no more call to bite you or me than we have to bite an elephant. Of course, did an elephant *step* on either of us, unexpected, we'd likely do whatever we could to it, and all a snake has to work with is its fangs. We know where he is and he knows where we are, so there's nothing to worry about."

She stared down at him in wonder as she said flatly, "Yesterday I saw you kill a man, Custis."

"I'm sorry about that. I try to avoid such displays of temper, even when ladies ain't present. It was the other gent's notion to shoot it out, not mine."

"*Ja*, but just the same, you shot him down like a dog, und now you say you're afraid to kill a *snake?*"

He shook his head. "You must not pay much attention to your surroundings, Herta. In the first place, I never shoot *dogs*, unless they come at me mad and frothing. The man I gunned by the stage station was worse than most mad dogs. He was a killer who knew just what he was doing, not a poor brute driven by sickness. As to yonder snake in the grass, he's just a poor brute, too, who means us no harm. I ain't *afraid* to kill him. I just have no sensible *reason* to. I figure the Good Lord had His reasons for putting critters of every kind on this earth. As long as snakes stick to killing mice and rabbits, I'm willing to live and let live, see?"

She shook her head again. *"Nein,* I *don't* see. I just asked you to spare our Hansel und you told me it was not your business if he lived or died."

He looked up at the sky and said, "I got some canned beans and tomatoes. We'd best eat something before it gets too hot." He rolled over to fumble the cans out of his possibles bag.

"What kind of an answer ist das?" she protested.

He got out his pocketknife to open the cans. "The only kind there can be, for a man deputized to uphold the law as the law in its infinite wisdom calls the shots. Hans Krinke's been charged with counterfeiting and jailbreak, on both sides of the water. He may or may not be innocent. My modest badge don't give me the right to judge him. That's up to a jury of his peers, once he's been brought in for a fair trial."

She sobbed. *"Ach, Gott,* do you think he'll get a fair trial in Vienna?"

He handed her a can. "Eat beans first and wash 'em down with the tomatoes. It's more complicated the other way. I'm sorry I ain't got a spoon for you, but canned goods is runny enough to drink from the tin."

She threw the can of beans as hard and as far as she could, cursing in German.

He shrugged. "Suit yourself. But that's sure a dumb way to eat beans."

She started to cry, said she was sorry, and asked if

47

there was any other way to change his mind about her Hansel. He handed her a can of tomatoes and warned, "Don't throw *this* one away. I didn't bring all that much grub along. I don't want to argue about my duties with you no more, Miss Herta. It's like arguing Karl Marx or any other religion. You got your mind set and I got my mind set. Let's talk about the weather. Ain't it hot this morning?"

She laughed through her tears and said, "Too hot it ist to *bear* und I fear we'll have no shade at all by noon!"

He glanced up through the overhead leaves. "There's no argument about that, at least. I sure wish you were a boy, Miss Herta. For if you wasn't built so delicate, by now I'd be out of these tweed pants and, come noon and no shade, I might just dip myself entire in that pool, yonder."

She glanced the same way and said with a sigh, *"Ja, so inviting das spring water looks, even early in the day. But could you naked swim in it, even if I was not here? What if someone else were to come along?"*

He asked, "Who? Not even the snakes are dumb enough to move far from shade at this time of the year, and we're miles from the nearest human settlement. Why don't you at least take that heavy skirt off? You're wearing underclothes, ain't you?"

She blushed and said, "Of course. But a gentlemen ist not supposed to mention a lady's unmentionables."

He shrugged and ate some beans. She finished her tomatoes, wiped her mouth, and decided, *"Ach, Gott,* so hot it ist, und *you* are not as dressed for the occasion. If I got out of this heavy skirt, just what would you think of me, Custis?"

He said he would think she was acting sensible for a change.

She shyly slipped out of her heavy velvet skirts. He didn't see what she had to be so shy about. Her damned old frilly pantaloons came down almost to her knees, and she was wearing black silk stockings above her low-cut riding boots. She leaned back with a luxurious sigh, saying, *"Ach, Gott,* so good that feels." But a few minutes later she complained about the heat again.

Longarm couldn't blame her. He was starting to itch under his pants, and it was still too hot for the parts of him that weren't.

"We got mayhaps a few more hours of shade," he said. "We'll feel better around noon if we're rested better. So here's what we'd best do. We'd best refill the canteens first. Then we can splash about in the pool and get cooled off enough to catch some shuteye before the noonday heat wakes us up for another dip."

She blinked and asked, "Are you serious? Do I look like a lady who naked with strange men swimming goes?"

He started to point out that he had meant they could paddle about in their underclothes, of course. Then he wondered why any man would want to say a dumb thing like that. So he grinned and said, "Well, hell, you can turn your *back* to me, can't you?"

She told him it was out of the question. So he lit another smoke. He asked her if she wanted a drag on his cheroot. She said she was so hot she was going to faint any minute. He nodded, rose, and picked up the depleted canteens to refill, while there was still some shade at the edge of the pool. He hunkered down to do so, noting that the water was clear now. The water felt

49

good on his bare feet as he refilled the canteens. He heard a wail of mortal female distress and then Herta passed him at a dead run, stark naked, to dive headfirst into the inviting water hole.

He chuckled and recapped the canteens before he rose to carry them back by the bedroll. He saw that her duds were scattered helter-skelter from there to the edge of the pool. She was splashing about in the middle of it, her red hair slicked to her skull as she laughed and announced for the whole world to hear that something was a wonder bar.

It still looked more like a muddy old water hole than a saloon to Longarm. But he dropped his pants and stepped out of them to take his own running dive into the water as well. It was a delightful shock to his flushed flesh, even though it was warmer than it should have been, thanks to the way water held heat after sundown. He swam underwater for a spell, opening his eyes. He saw Herta's slender but curvaceous body ahead of him. He surfaced near her, losing a lot of scenery in the exchange, even though her face was pretty as a picture, smiling at him. She said, "Oh, I am so glad you talked me into this, Custis. Even out here in the full sunlight it feels like in heaven we are, *nicht wahr?*"

He agreed it beat sunstroke. She laughed and dove under like a sea lion, exposing a patch of pale rump for a split second. He had already seen more than that underwater and he knew if *she* swam underwater with her eyes open she would see more of him than Queen Victoria might consider proper. From the way she was blushing when she came up for air, he knew she had. But she never let on. They went on splashing like kids

50

till his own goose bumps and her shivers told him they were overdoing it.

So it seemed only natural for him to take her in his arms and carry her out of the pool, and just as natural to lay her atop the bedroll in the shade and proceed to do what came natural.

Afterwards, they fell asleep in each other's arms. They got a few hours' sleep before the sun woke them up again. They walked hand in hand back into the water hole and this time they wound up making love in the shallows. They stayed in the water for a couple of hours, to get out wrinkled as well as a mite sunburned. Her paler hide had suffered more from the sun than Longarm's, of course, but they got around it by letting her do it on top before they went back to sleep for a few hours, now that the shade was back, slanted the other way.

The next time they woke up it was getting dark and they had to make love again to calm their goose bumps. Then, despite her protests about it being too early, he made her get dressed, hauling on his own duds as he explained, "We've lost almost an hour's travel time as it is, oversleeping sundown and acting weak-natured. Do you know how to find the north star, Herta?"

She said everyone knew how to do that.

"You'd be surprised," he said. "I once had to track down an army patrol led by an officer who got all the way through West Point without knowing the Big Dipper from his elbow. If you keep the north star over your left shoulder as much as you can, you ought to make out the lights of Rosebud Wash long before you get there. If you find yourself an on open desert at sunrise, you'll know you missed it. Drape your saddle blanket over

51

some sagebrush and crawl under it until it gets dark again. Then head back the other way and hope for the best. You got enough water to last you seventy-two hours, if you hold out as long as you can between sips, and sip small."

She asked about her horse.

He said, "Oh, he'll drop on you in less'n forty-eight whether you water him or not. So don't water him. You'd be surprised how far your own two feet can carry you, if you got water and only travel at night. I don't expect you to get lost. I'm just making sure you know what to do if you manage to. Got any other questions?"

"*Ja,* I am frightened und I wish to go on with you."

"That ain't a question. It's pure impossible, and you know it. Ask something sensible."

She asked whether he would be coming back by way of Rosebud Wash and tried to get him to promise not to shoot her fellow Marxist. He told her he'd look her up if he ever made it back this way, and assured her he had no intention of gunning her infernal Hansel.

She kissed him good and let him put her on her stud. Then she leaned down to kiss him again before she rode off into the dark, crying fit to bust.

He saddled his own mules, cast a last wistful glance at the moonlit water hole, and mounted up, muttering, "Lord knows what I'll do if I get back to Rosebud Wash to find both Herta and Babs waiting for me. Of course, if I have to gun old Hansel, Herta likely won't want to screw me no more, in any case."

Chapter 4

The moonlit slopes of Skull Mesa loomed above them as Longarm found the big boulder Bull Culhane had mentioned. One look told him how the mesa had gotten its name and that the older lawman had only given him hearsay directions. The barn-sized dome of pumice looked like a giant human skull, buried to the cheekbones and staring at him, unfriendly as hell. He didn't have time to determine whether the cavernous eyeholes were natural or enthusiastic vandalism. The trail he had followed from the water hole to here forked in front of him as Culhane had said it might.

The recent dust-up had erased any sign as might have been on either choice. But it was easy to see the one to his left was three times as wide and wheel-rutted. The moonlit trail leading off to the north was little more than a bridle path cutting through the stirrup-high sage. But Longarm still hesitated as he patted his mount and asked it, "Why would there be a trail at all if it didn't *go* nowheres, mule? I sure wish we had the time for some scouting. But we don't. The wagons would have gone *that* way, so we'll say no more about it."

The mules were in no position to argue. An hour and six or eight miles later, Skull Mesa was still keeping company with them on their right. For it was a bigger rise than it had looked head-on. There was no end to it in sight, ahead, and Longarm knew that in this corner of the Great Basin the wetter winds came from the north. So he frowned and asked aloud, "How come that old Indian said this was the best way if the other side has to be catching such rain as might pass this way?"

He went over the whole tale again in his head as they pressed on. Then he nodded to himself and muttered, "Right. He said it was a *salty* trail, not a *dry* one."

The curse of the basin and range country was ancient geography as much as current climate. The Great Basin got almost as much rain as the High Plains east of the Rockies. But the soil of the High Plains was sweet enough for thrifty short-grass. So such rain as there was tended to soak into the soil for later use by the same. It didn't work that way out here. For, millions of years ago, there'd been a salt sea in these parts. A lot of the jaggedy ranges thrust skyward by some trick of nature were made of rock that had once been muddy sea bottom or underwater lava reefs. The rock was hard and bare now, so rainwater ran off many a slope the way it ran off a tin roof. And a lot of the old sea salt and water-soluble volcano-crud was still in the rock to taint the running water, if only a mite.

A mite each rain was enough, when the water had no place to run to. Not a river or a dry-wash in the Great Basin had any outlet to the sea. So for many a mostly dry year the tainted runoff had just dried up, leaving its witch-brewed chemistry behind to poison the earth. The sweetwater pool he had shared with Herta had been one of the rare spots where the water drained more reasonable rock. Sage and cheat grass could grow in soil too alkaline for most plants. Salt weed was even tougher and indicated it was a pure waste of time to drill a well to the water table. There were other places where nothing at all could grow, and the summer sun baking down all day on naked soil, rock, or salt flat didn't do a thing to cool the desert winds.

By midnight he had seen the last of Skull Mesa and was crossing a big sage flat. Culhane had warned him there would be no water for a full night's ride. But mules didn't work like that. So he stopped and put a quart of canteen water and a couple of fistfuls of oats in each mule's feed bag. It wouldn't have been enough for horses, and the mules protested it wasn't enough for them, but he knew better. He swapped saddles and rode on after a fifteen-minute trail break.

The rest of the night was as tedious as the wagon trace they were following, broken by an occasional mild surprise to speculate on. By four o'clock he started spotting things along the trail cast aside by the wagon train he was tracking. He knew it had to be them, littering the desert with cast-iron pots, grandfather clocks, and such, because the dust hadn't buried anything deep enough to matter. It seemed a mite early for them to be tossing away expensive gear. They had surely filled their water kegs as well as their oxen back at that last sweetwater, and Culhane had said there was water dead ahead as well.

There was. The mules smelled it just as the sky was pearling light behind them. He didn't let them run the last mile, tempting as it was. So it was light enough to see colors by the time they burst out of the sage into about five acres of trampled mud with a half-acre pond in the middle of it. Longarm was glad he could see so well as he reined in by the water's edge. He growled, "Oh, suffering snakes, there ought to be a law!"

The fools on the trail ahead of him had put out their campfire by kicking the burning remains into the pond, no doubt to improve the water quality. They had let their livestock crap along the edges and, worse yet, a pile of human excrement told him where someone had squatted at the last before he or she no doubt ran on to catch up.

He let the mules drink. He would have had a time stopping them. But he refreshed himself with tepid, tinny canteen water as he pondered his next moves.

There was a bentwood rocker, a brass bedstead, and a pot-bellied stove abandoned near the water hole. It had likely been too much effort to shove the stuff into the water. The same could not be said for empty cans and a liquor bottle bobbing out in the middle. He grimaced and told the mules, "They've been pushing too hard. We're a good thirty miles from that last water hole. So they'd have made camp smack between 'em if they had any desert savvy. It looks like the sun caught 'em in the open and they pushed on anyway. It's no wonder they seem to have had a swimming party and breakfast at the same time."

He dismounted and left the mules drinking the dirty water, knowing neither would drift off from the water even at gunpoint, now that the sun was rising. He followed the trail beyond the water hole to where it burst through a wall of greasewood and headed straight out across bare earth as flat and hard as brick. He sighed and said, "Well, they said this water hole lay at the edge of the Black Rock Desert."

He wasn't about to follow the tracks across in desert daylight. He went back to the abandoned campsite. The mules had had enough water, but one was trying to ruin Longarm's McClellan saddle and bedroll by wallowing in the water like an infernal hippo. He waded in, hauled it out, and unsaddled it. The other came over like a friendly pup for the same favor. He hauled the riding and pack saddles into the brush, well clear of the dirty campsite. Then he broke out a short-handled spade and proceeded to dig a knee-deep hole. He quit when he saw the sides were moist. It would take some time for the seepage to amount to much. Meanwhile, if that French chemist was right about the little bugs he said caused fevers, they'd have a chore wriggling a good hundred yards from the dirty water hole.

He knew the mules could make it through the day without shade as long as they had water to drink and wallow in. That left himself to worry about. He dragged the old bedstead over and tented his cover tarp over the brass. Then he spread his ground cloth under it, got undressed, and stretched out naked in the improvised shade.

It worked. He hadn't had as much sleep the past two days as he'd planned on. So in no time at all he was back in Denver, playing slap and tickle with that widow woman up on Sherman Avenue as she fed him lemonade. Then he somehow got to dreaming about a she-devil trying to get him to screw her in hell on a hot bed of coals and, since he didn't want to, he woke up.

It was as hot as he'd been dreaming, now, but he saw the sun was low to the west. He didn't try to go back to sleep. He sat up to make sure his mules were still there as well as alive. They were. He hauled on his boots, picked up his Winchester and the empty canteens, and moseyed over to his private water hole to see how it was doing.

It had seeped full of water that looked clear and clean but smelled and tasted like someone had done laundry in it, using plenty of soap. Culhane had said it was safe water, though. He filled his canteens and then splashed some all over his bare hide. He was dry again by the time he got back under his improvised canopy, but he felt a mite better. He ate and smoked and then smoked some more until it got dark enough to travel.

He swapped saddles again, of course, but the mules still gave him an argument when they saw he meant to take them away from the water. He didn't get sore at them. He knew they'd be fighting even harder if they knew where they were really going.

The Black Rock Desert would have been a lake, a big one, under a more generous sky. As it was, there were years when the whole vast playa lay under a few inches of water from late winter to early spring. But the one modest river running into the big sink from the north couldn't keep it filled against the summer sun and bone-dry desert wind. So it took turns being too wet for desert brush and too dry for water lilies. The results were sun-baked, bare adobe, thirty-odd miles across where it was skinny.

At night, even with the full moon shining, it was impossible to see the Black Rock Mountains above the far shore. But the trail was easy enough to follow. Aside from recent sign, there were smoothed-out ruts from many a wagon of the heavier traffic during the Paiute troubles. By the time he had ridden a few hours out, Longarm was certain he'd have preferred to take his chances with the Paiutes.

From time to time he spied more abandoned baggage. Before midnight he came upon what was left of an ox that hadn't been able to stagger on. They'd had the sense to butcher it, at least. It was still a mite early for even oxen to give out. He wondered why it had.

About halfway across—he hoped—Longarm found another campsite. That made sense, figuring fifteen miles as a night's haul for oxen.

He dismounted to rest his own livestock and see if he could read any sign. He found a big flower pot with a pathetic baby lilac still rooted in the dried-out potting soil. He nodded and said aloud, "I'm sure sorry, ma'am. It must have hurt to leave a reminder of home behind.

59

But you'll find lots of lilac in Oregon, if only you make it."

There was other abandoned gear and not as much dung. That was a bad sign. You had to keep oxen watered well enough to crap every few minutes if you expected them to keep pulling. It must have been hot and dry as hell out here, even under the wagon hoods, and of course the brutes wouldn't be inside the wagons.

Not wishing to share the experience, Longarm watered his mules and pressed on, taking advantage of the cool night air to trot them as much as common sense and an eye to the future called for. He knew that while the Black Rock was dramatic desert, it wasn't the last or even a good part of the desert to be crossed this side of Fort Bidwell.

Around three in the morning he spied a distant pinpoint of light, too close to the ground to pass for a star. His first thought was that he'd caught up with that wagon train at last. But that couldn't be, for two good reasons. In the first place, the emigrants would be traveling, not camping, in the cool dark. In the second place the light was way the hell north of the trail, unless the trail curved a lot ahead. That made little sense on dead flat open playa. But in case the trail *was* laid out in a curve, Longarm swung off it to make for the distant beacon. Someone was camped there, sure as hell, and if it wasn't the party he was searching for, they might at least know the country ahead better.

Distances were deceptive in desert country, as many a pilgrim had discovered before he died of thirst. The sun was threatening to rise again by the time Longarm got to the stone cabin, built in the mouth of a canyon running into the barren slopes behind it, and saw that the light he'd been chasing all this time came from an oil lamp on the sill of an open window.

As he rode on in, a side door opened to spill more light, and a gruff male voice called out, "We see you coming, stranger. Afore you come any closer, you'd best state your name and business."

The gent in the doorway was holding a long-range buffalo gun at port. There were times when it paid to tell the truth and there were times when it might get a lawman killed. Longarm called back, "I answer to anything you'd like to call me but late-for-breakfast. I've been chasing a wagon train up the Siwash Trail without much luck. If I ain't lost, where the hell might I be?"

The man in the doorway called back, "You're right. You're lost. The trail you want runs a good eight or ten miles to the south, such as it is."

Another form appeared in the doorway to whisper something and the one with the rifle announced, "We can show you a short cut through the mountains ahint us. But it'll cost you."

"How much?" Longarm asked.

"Ten dollars for pointing the way. Dollar a gallon for such water as you may need."

"Ain't that a mite steep for water, friend?"

"Not out here. We're sitting on the only water for a day's ride in any fool direction. If you can't afford water, you need directions even more. For our cutoff will save you a good forty miles of mighty serious traveling."

"All I got on me is eight dollars and change," Longarm called back. "But I can see you got me by the short hairs, so can I owe you the rest?"

The man in the doorway laughed. Longarm had

wanted him to. That was why he'd stretched the truth a mite. Bully boys were always more cheerful when they thought they had the edge on you. The man in the doorway said, "Come on in and have some coffee, free. We'll decide whether to skin you or not after we hears your tale."

Longarm rode on in, dismounted, and said, "Got to comfort my critters before I coffee myself, pard."

At closer range the rifleman was young and rat-faced, with a week's growth of beard and army pants. It was a dragoon outfit, judging from the paler blue stripes down the legs. From the waist up he wore an undershirt and had a dire need for soap and water. "Our squaw can tend to your critters," he said. "What was that name again?"

"Washington," Longarm lied, "Booker T. Washington."

"Ain't there a famous black man with a similar name?"

"So they tell me. I'm from the less famous side of the family."

The young ruffian laughed and told him to come on in. As he did so, a skinny Digger Indian woman, dressed skimpy even for a Digger, eased past them to tend to the mules. Longarm met another, somewhat older gent inside. He was seated at a pine table under a greasy hat inside a sun-faded army issue shirt. "Sit down," he said. "The squaw will coffee you in a minute, if she knows what's good for her."

Longarm sat on a nail keg across from his surly host, not letting on as he took in his surroundings. The stone walls were neatly lined with hand-hewn shelves holding canned goods and even some books. Some mining tools stood in a corner, their handles lashed together with twine and the metal dusty but well-oiled and rust-free. He said, "I can see you boys have been working color, here. I don't blame you for being cautious. But don't worry. I ain't in the prospecting business."

The one who had led him in took another seat, so they had him in a crossfire. "What business *are* you in, Booker T. Washington?" he asked flatly.

Longarm smiled sheepishly. "I plays cards, now and again. I don't suppose you boys would like to work out our financial dealing with a little friendly card game? Your deck, of course."

They both laughed sneeringly. The older one said, "Right, you're a tinhorn they run outten Rosebud Wash, no doubt for dealing from your *own* friendly deck. You don't look strong enough to dig for gold. We'll show you how to punch through the hills to the trail your pals took, and we'll even water you. But it'll cost you all your cash and that frock coat you're wearing."

"I could use that Stetson, too," his younger comrade decided.

Longarm frowned thoughtfully.

The older one said, "I'll let you have this hat I'm wearing in exchange. I ain't so unChristian as to send a man out in the desert with no hat at all."

Before Longarm could answer, the Digger woman came back in, looking wild-eyed and scared. The younger one slapped her bare rump as she edged past him to get at the coffee pot on the stove. The older one noted the way Longarm was taking the exchange and said with a lewd grin, "It's too bad you didn't bring along much money. She screws mighty fine, and it'd cost you less than water."

The other one laughed. "Water's harder to find out here than Diggers. That's why she can't run off on us, see?"

Longarm did. "I was wondering if her arrangement with you boys was willing or otherwise, he said. "Now that I see it ain't, I see no further point in this discussion. You boys is both under arrest. Whether you want to come quiet or otherwise is up to you."

They both started to move at once but froze as Longarm snapped, "Don't," in a no-nonsense voice.

The one behind the table smiled innocently and asked, "What are you, some sort of Injun lover, Booker T.?"

Longarm said, "I'm federal law, and you've been loving Indians more than federal laws allow. Aside from that, when we all get up to Fort Bidwell I feel sure your recent supply sergeant will want them duds you deserted in back, dirty as they may be right now."

The one behind the table slowly began to edge his hands back across the greasy pine. He snorted in disbelief. "Now whatever gave you the notion we was solider boys, Sheriff?" he asked.

Longarm said, "I ain't no sheriff, and you two are piss-poor excuses for soldiers. But it ain't too hard to read the sign here. This miner's cabin is neat and clean, or was, till you two pigs moved in with a squaw you'd enslaved along the way. You're both wearing army duds. Dragoon. The only dragoon outfit within sensible distance is posted up at Fort Bidwell. Lucky for you, that's where I was headed in any case. It's too light out, now, to leave this shade. So I reckon I'll just have to cuff you together till it's time to move on. You can show

64

me your cutoff through the mountains after sundown, unless you want to wind up thirsty as hell. For I've no water to spare a stubborn child, even at a dollar a gallon."

It would have worked that way, had not the confused Digger gal turned from the stove just then, coffee pot in hand, and confused things more by asking something in her own dialect. Longarm glanced her way without thinking. It was the chance the one behind the table had been waiting for.

But sitting at a table worked both ways, and Longarm had his own .44 out before he'd begun the argument. So he only had to pull the trigger, an' double-action did the rest.

As the heavy-set one flew backwards, chair and all, the little squaw threw the hot coffee from her pot in the other one's face as he was swinging his buffalo gun's muzzle up to blow Longarm away. Longarm pivoted on the keg top and put a round of .44-40 in him. As he slid to the floor, coffee-stained as well as dead, the Indian girl fell to her knees and wailed, "No hurt Tocmetone!"

Longarm loomed to his feet in the haze of gunsmoke and moved around to make sure of the first one on the far side of the table. "Cut the fussing, girl," he told her. "Nobody's about to hurt you, now."

She grabbed his leg and hugged it like a long-lost child as she pleaded, "Hear me, I am not a bad person. I throw coffee because Jake point gun at you. I know thinkum. Everyone say Tocmetone dumb as hell."

He saw that the older deserter was dead, too, so he reloaded, feeling foolish with the Indian girl clinging to his legs like that. "Cut that out," he told her. "The war's over. I work for the Great White Father and I mean to take you back to your agency as soon as it's cool enough to travel."

She looked up blankly and asked, "Agency?"

He sighed. "Right. Your band is still unreconstructed, albeit likely harmless. You can tell me about it after I get rid of our cadavers. They'll stink like hell in no time, hot as it figures to get in here by noon."

She rose to her feet. "I know good place. Saltu miners dig big hole in ground up canyon, *ka?*"

He shook his head. "That would hardly be Christian, no offense. I can see, by the provisions all around, this place has only been left vacant during the hot summer months. I'd hate like hell to find two dead men in *my* mine shaft come November."

He holstered his revolver, took off his coat, and bent to grab the corpse nearest the door by the booted ankles. As he had expected, it was already hot outside. He saw that his mules had been tethered under a nearby lean-to, along with two bay army horses. He knew there was a spade lashed to his pack saddle. He knew how hot it was as well. So he dragged the younger deserter out onto the open playa a ways before he let go of the boots, patted the corpse down for I.D. and seventy-eight cents, and told it, "That'll hold you. By fall anything the buzzards leave of you will be too dried out to stink."

As he started back, he saw Tocmetone had the heavier one by the heels and was treating him to the same informal funeral. She was stronger than she looked. He moved to help her. They put the second cadaver neatly by the first one and it was good for another dollar and six bits. As he put the I.D. away for the army, Longarm

66

told the girl, "It was small wonder they was so desperate for money as well as civilian duds. They likely just lucked on to that cabin and knew better than to go on. If they knew about Rosebud Wash they knew the desert hereabouts as well. Do you know the way to the Siwash Trail, Tocmetone?"

She shook her head. "*Ka*, my people Ho, not Siwash. Me never meetum any Siwash. They bad or good?"

He said, "Never mind. Let's get out of this sun before we fry."

As he led her back to the cabin he asked her if she at least knew where she had been recently. It stood to reason the army deserters had followed *some* damned trail down here from Fort Bidwell, since their ponies were still alive.

Tocmetone said, "I findem water for they. They lost when they catch me alone in hills and screw me crazy. Them bad ones too rough. Even *hit* for no reason. Why you thinkem they so rough? Me know better than to fight with *men*."

They went inside. He told her she could call him Custis if she put more coffee on. She did and he told her to let the fire go out as soon as they had a big potful perked. It was already getting stuffy inside, despite the stone walls. The cabin had been built for winter, not summer, so the doors and windows all faced southwest, to catch as much sun as they could.

It seemed overly polite as well as stupid to stay fully dressed in the company of a stark naked woman who no doubt had primitive motions of proper dress in any case. He still felt a mite awkward as he undressed and hung

67

his duds up. He left his underdrawers on. She asked how come as she poured his coffee and suggested, "It too hot to screw in little while, Custis."

He told her it was already too hot, not wanting to hurt her feelings. Longarm had practical reservations. He opened a can of beans to share with her and told her, "I can't leave you here and I got places to go, Tocmetone."

"Good," she said. "Wherever you go, me go, too."

He said, "I ain't sure your folks would approve, Tocmetone. I know the army would raise pure ned, and ask how come you were still running loose, if I took you in to Fort Bidwell in that costume. Don't you have any notion where your own band might be right now?"

She said, "Sure. Me not *that* stupid. This time of year Ho up in hills, gathering pine nuts, bitter roots, and other good things. But why *you* want to go there? You Saltu don't *like* bitter root."

He chuckled. "You're right. I've eaten it, but it tastes awful. My plan is to carry you back to your own band before I search further for the wagon train I'm trailing. I'm losing time I can't afford, but I'm duty-bound to restore you to your own people. By the way, where did you learn to talk English so good, if your band ain't come in yet?"

She washed down some beans with coffee and explained, "My father, Ocheoe, cousin of Keintpoos. You Saltu callem Captain Jack."

"Jesus Christ, are you a *Modoc,* girl?"

She shrugged. "I am Ho. All of us are Ho, no matter what *you* call us. Tocmetone not know why you call us different nations and shoot some of us while you teach others to read. Anyway, seven summers ago my band

68

live at mission west of Fort Bidwell. We not evil people. We try to learn Saltu ways. Then some Saltu say band of Keintpoos killem Saltu. It big lie. All real Ho know *Shasta* band do this thing. When soldiers try to punish wrong Ho, Keintpoos you call Captain Jack go crazy and try to fight whole army. My father say, better we go someplace else. So we do. Since then we hide from everbody. Bad soldiers who screwed me caught me gathering roots alone. My people very scared, *before* soldiers steal me. I think they kill you if I take you there. Better I don't. I have spoken."

He shook his head. "No, you ain't. In the first place, I ain't about to abandon a naked girl child in this desert. In the second, it's about time your old man heard the latest news, before he gets in trouble. The Modoc war has been over for years. The Paiutes are at peace and getting fat on B.I.A. rations. I can't ask your band to come in. But the least I can do is tell 'em they ain't at war with anyone."

He looked outside, swore softly, and said, "We'd best catch some sleep. Come nightfall, we'll talk some more about finding your band."

She shrugged and said, "You crazy. You wantem die. Why you so crazy, Custis?"

He sighed. "I don't know. I reckon it just comes natural with the job."

Chapter 5

They had ridden most of the night, Tocmetone leading the extra army pony home as added coup. Longarm was now so turned around he was beginning to suspect she didn't know where they were, either. The moonlit lava boulders all about all looked the same, and if they were on a trail he couldn't see it from the saddle. They topped a rise and she led him down into a draw shaded black as ink. He was about to call out something suspicious when he heard a male voice shouting, *"Ot-we-kau-tux-ee!"*

Longarm went for his saddle gun, but his guide yelled, *"Ka, ka!"* like an angry crow. Longarm knew that meant "no" in Ho. So despite the war cry, the Indians materializing from the black rocks all around began to act nicer as Tocmetone began to tell them her tale.

A naked Ho grabbed Longarm's reins and announced, "You don't get to die, after all. Hear me, I am Washoke, brother of Tocmetone. She says you have not bothered her even once. That is good. I know my sister is beautiful, but I would have had to kill you, had you bothered her."

Longarm replied that he had resisted the considerable temptation with something like that in mind. Washoke nodded soberly and said, "We men understand one another, even Ho and Saltu."

The Indians took him into their camp, hidden among the rocks deeper in the draw. He wasn't as surprised as some whites might have been to see substantial grass-thatched shelters. He knew that what his own kind called the Digger Indian culture was due more to necessity than invention. The widespread, vaguely related people who called themselves the Ho, or People, were opportunists who took life as conditions called for. Put a Ho in horse country and he'd soon steal a horse and turn into a Shoshone or Comanche. Put him where corn grew well, and he didn't have to move constantly, and he would build a pueblo and turn into a Hopi. Out on barren desert where neither corn nor anything much bigger than a jackrabbit could grow, he just as quickly turned into a despised "Digger Indian," even though a man had to be smart as hell to find anything to eat or drink in the Basin and Range country.

Tocmetone's band was living somewhere between true Digger and the more advanced mountain tribes farther west. They ran about naked because they would have suffocated wearing buckskins and war bonnets. But more than one brave had a new repeating rifle, and Longarm suspected he might have stumbled over them just in time.

He talked about that to Tocmetone's father, old Ocheoe, as they sat on a blanket and took turns on a calabash pipe Ocheoe was proud of.

Ocheoe calmed down once Longarm assured him that since he wasn't with the B.I.A. it was none of his business whether the band stayed wild or took up knitting. When asked about the old Indian who had died in Rosebud Wash full of Paiute arrows, the band leader shrugged. "I did not know the man. He as not from our band. The times were very confusing. Your people have my people all mixed up. You are always punishing the wrong Ho."

Longarm nodded, but said, "No offense, but you seem mixed up at times as well. Ain't it true the Horse Utes are Ho, even though they kill other Ho on sight?"

Ocheoe shrugged again. "Hear me, you Saltu seem to be all one people," he said. "Yet a few years ago those who wore gray killed those who wore blue on sight. We real people have the right to blood feuds, too, don't we? You should tell the Great White Father to get us straight. You give unrelated bands the same names. You call people of the same clan by different names."

"I've noticed that. Can we get back to the man called Siwash? I never saw the arrows he'd been hit with. Could *you* tell a Paiute arrow from, say, a Shoshone?"

The older man shook his head. "It would depend on the arrow maker, not his band. An arrow is an arrow. One makes an arrow out of what one has to work with. On the High Plains to the east some nations paint their arrow shafts differently to let their enemies know who killed them. We Ho don't do that. We don't care what our enemies think, as long as they are dead."

Longarm nodded and said, "In other words, that old wounded man could have belonged to almost any Ho nation, and been shot in battle, or just because someone didn't like him."

Ocheoe nodded. "Maybe he took the wrong woman, or maybe someone thought he was making bad medicine. I think he had to be a true Ho, though. From one of the bands you call Diggers."

"How do you know that, my elder brother?"

"He knew the country. He was able to tell of more than one trail. Can't you people figure anything out without help?"

"Right. He couldn't have ridden *both* trails coming in with mortal arrows in his hide. He knew where to ride for medical attention, too, even if it didn't do him much good. My elder brother is wise. He was a local Digger who got jumped by a band of mayhaps Horse Utes. He somehow managed to steal one of their ponies, and—"

"You are still talking silly," the Indian cut in. "You say the horse he rode bareback was *shod*. Have you ever met a Ute blacksmith?"

Longarm said, "As a matter of fact, I have. I know an Arapaho dentist in Denver, as well. But we agreed not to argue about the advantages of coming in. Your point's well took. The wounded Ho must have stole a white man's horse somewhere. That's a little late to worry about. During the Paiute troubles there was lots of livestock run off. All that's important is that the old man knew the best way across and told *our* side about

74

it. Do *you* know the trail we're talking about, elder brother?"

"Not to the east," Ocheoe said. "We do not roam that far. I know where your wagon party is. When wagons are rolling through one's hunting grounds, it is a good idea to keep an eye on them. So we have been. If you want, I can have one of my young men show you the way."

Longarm looked up at the sky. "It's getting late to travel, ain't it?" he observed.

"As sensible people travel, yes," the Indian said. "But that wagon train has been traveling by day. If you leave now, you may catch up by noon."

Longarm nodded, but said soberly, "Suffering snakes, it's no *wonder* they've been leaving lilac pots behind!"

The guide the Indians gave him seemed friendly enough but spoke not a word of English. Longarm knew but a few words of Ho and the complex grammar escaped him entirely. So the first leg of their ride was sort of tedious, as well as mighty hot once the sun was up.

It would have been hotter if the Ho ahead of him, on an unshod paint, had not stuck as much as possible to the high ground. They rode along rocky ridges through a thrifty cover of piñon and juniper that at least smelled cooler than the sun-baked, salt-tolerant brush on the flats below. But as the sun rose higher, even altitude began to fail them. Longarm's mount spooked at what sounded like a pistol shot and the Indian guide turned to say something reassuring. Longarm nodded and said,

"Ride on, old son. I've heard the desert sun split rocks before."

It was surprising how two men who didn't understand each other's words could understand each other. The young Ho laughed and rode on, and the next time a glassy lump of black rock went off, he didn't even look back.

Longarm saw that they were aiming for a peak farther up the ridge. His guide hooted like a sunstruck owl bird as they moved up the final slope and another Ho materialized among the black boulders of the lookout. The guide explained what he was doing up here with a white man and the scout explained, in fair mission English, "The wagons you hunt are still in sight. Come. I will show you."

Longarm and his guide dismounted. The three of them moved up to the lookout, from where one could see clear across the dead-flat basin to the northwest. The scout pointed due west at nothing much and said, "That is where they were at dawn, circled up as if they knew we were watching. I wonder what they would do if we built a smudge fire and sent up some smoke. It might be fun."

"I sure wish you wouldn't," Longarm said. "He swept north with his eyes and finally spotted a dotted line of bitty ants crawling ever so slowly across the furnace floor. "Why do you people camp when it is cool and move when it is hot?" the scout asked. "Are you trying to test your medicine, or simply stupid?"

Longarm said, "*Some* of us know better. How far are the wagons from the next water?"

"Good water?" the Indian said. "A night's travel, as they are moving. They will come to bad water before that. About sundown, I would say. For some reason, an earlier wagon party dug for water there and found it, not too deep. I don't know why. Anyone can see that whole basin is covered with salt bush. We ate good that summer. The alkali did not hurt the meat of the poisoned stock they left along the trail for us."

Longarm nodded grimly and said, "I hate to be the one to have to tell you this, but I aim to leave less carrion for you and the buzzards, if it's all the same to you."

They were good sports about it. They wished him well, even if he *was* crazy, as he remounted and headed down the slope to cut the wagon train's course at an angle. It was as easy for a mule to slope downhill as it was to stiff-leg against the pull, so he let them. They did raise some dust and the white folk out on the flat did see it, so long before he reached them, Longarm saw that they were circling the wagons again. He snorted in disgust and rode for the hastily improvised little fort of wood and canvas. As he got within about half a mile, gunsmoke blossomed from between two wagons and a buffalo slug whizzed high and wide to his right. He couldn't tell if it was a warning shot or just poor shooting. He waved his Stetson over his head and rode on as he bellowed, "Hold your fire, damn your blind eyes! Do I look like a damned old war party?"

Nobody else fired as he rode on in and through a gap in the wagons. He reined in sharp, to keep from riding over anybody, and stared down in disgust at the dusty, scared faces staring back up at him. There were too many men, women, and children to shake a stick at. The livestock milling about in the center of the wagon ring didn't do a thing to ease the crowded conditions, even though most of the mounts and at least half the oxen looked brighter than the emigrants all trying to babble at him at once.

Longarm drew his .44 and shot at the sky for silence. A baby began to wail like hell, but the shot shut everyone else up. He said, "That's more like it. Who's supposed to be in charge of this foolishness?"

A heavy-set, bearded man wearing a red calico shirt and packing his Colt '74 tucked into the waistband of his jeans announced, "This is the Purvis party, and I'd be head scout and wagonmaster, Silas Bradford. For, you see, I knows the Siwash Trail."

Longarm dismounted, told a willing looking kid to hold the reins for now, and told Bradford, "That's *all* you know, then. I'm Deputy U. S. Marshal Custis Long and, as of this minute, I'm taking command of this train."

Bradford put a hand on the grips of his '74 and snapped, "See here, I was hired to see these folk safe to Fort Bidwell, and that's what I aim to do. So you can just go to hell!"

"You've a fair chance of getting to hell sooner than you might have planned if you don't let go that gun, or *draw* it, good as your brag," Longarm told him.

Bradford seemed suddenly to lose interest in his pistol grips. But he went on scowling as a taller and older man in an undertaker's suit stepped between them to announce, "I am Dr. Richard Purvis, the elected captain of this cooperative Oregon adventure. So, you see, it is up to *me*, not *you*, to say who's in command here."

Longarm said, "You're wrong. You're all in mortal peril on desert owned by the federal government, and I'm the ranking federal official this side of Fort Bidwell.

So it's my duty to save you from your own suicidal tendencies, whether you want me to or not."

He turned back to Bradford. "Would you be one of the Bradford brothers contracted to run mail through these parts?" he asked.

The bearded wonder said he would be.

Longarm said, "They told me in Rosebud Wash you boys knew what you was doing. So what in thunder have you been trying to *do* to these folk? You have to know desert travel in high summer calls for day camps and night marches, not the other way around."

Bradford nodded, but said, "It can't be helped. We've been dogged by Injuns all the way. Everyone knows how hard it is to spy a Digger in the sage by broad daylight. Moving strung out in the dark would just be giving them our hair for free!"

Longarm snorted in disgust. "All right, everyone. I want you to forget everything this obvious escaped lunatic may have told you, up to now, and listen. Unless *you're* all crazy, too, you must have noticed it's at least a hundred and twenty in the sun right now, and every one of them oxen gives off as much heat as an oven. So I want you men to herd them outside on the double. They won't stray, knowing you got the water. The ground you're standing on is alkali, but the salt bush all about is harmless, and stock enjoys it.

"While the men herd the critters I want you women to herd yourselves and the kids up into the wagons and get as undressed as far as modesty and common sense allows. Anyone wearing more than underwear on a day like this ain't *got* much common sense. Anyone who feels flushed but clammy at the same time should lie down with a wet rag draped over his or her face, and breathe through the wet cloth. I'd wet down all the kids whether they look heat-struck or not. Don't nobody drink hard liquor. How much *water* you drink depends on how much you got. The next drinking water is eighteen hours ahead, so it's up to you, not me, to hoard your supplies."

He saw that nobody was moving. He turned to Bradford and snapped, "What are you waiting for? You know what I want you to do. So *do* it, *now,* or fill your fist. I don't mean to say that twice."

Bradford gulped and turned away, yelling, "All right, boys, you heard the lawman. Let's get them critters moving. He's right about salt bush, anyways."

As the others began to do his bidding, Longarm turned to take the reins of his lead mule, giving the kid who had been holding them a friendly pat as he told him to get out of the sun, too. The kid asked, "Are you sure them Injuns won't attack, mister?"

"I'll tell you a secret if you promise to keep it to yourself," Longarm said. "How many whites do you reckon Indians killed in the great gold rush year of Forty-nine, son?"

"Gee, I dunno. Thousands?" the kid said.

Longarm shook his head. "Thirty-three. You can look it up. I had to, one time, when a trigger-happy officer bet me a hundred bucks. The very worst year for wagon parties was 1850. That year the Indians between the Big Muddy and the West Coast killed a grand total of forty-eight whites, and we killed seventy-six of them. *Indians* have never been the problem out here, son. If you don't get that bare head under a wagon tarp, sudden, you'll wind up one of the *grimmer* statistics yourself, hear?"

The kid lit out as if the entire Lakota Nation were after him. Longarm began to unsaddle his mules. Purvis moved closer and said, "I can see you're used to handling men and boys. Were you an officer in the War?"

Longarm said, "As a matter of fact, I was a boy. I'm *looking* for an officer, though. You ever hear of an Austro–Hungarian colonel called Von Thaldorf?"

Purvis nodded. "He joined us just outside Rosebud Wash. I think you just chased him off with the livestock. Do you want me to send after him?"

Longarm shook his head. "He ain't likely to drift far, and we got a long, tedious day to kill, here. What about another foreigner, called Krinke?"

Purvis said, "Von Thaldorf told us about him. He overtook us in the hope the wanted criminal might have left for Fort Bidwell with us."

Longarm nodded. "Naturally, had the colonel caught up with Krinke, he wouldn't be out herding oxen for us right now. It's nice to know I guess right once in a while. But as long as I have your ear, I'd best turn over every wet rock. How do you and the colonel know Krinke ain't with you?"

"Are you mad? We just agreed the colonel would have arrested him on sight."

Longarm said, "Sure. So would I, if I *knew* him on sight. They wired me a description of Hans Krinke. He's so average-looking he makes me sick. White male, aged thirty-eight, five-foot-eleven, medium build, brown hair, and eyes either gray, hazel, or green. They must have took *that* down under artificial light. He's from a once aristocratic family, living in genteel poverty. Made it halfway through the university before he had to leave. Speaks good French and English, as well as German, of course. That's all she wrote. The colonel may have a better description, but according to my notes *he* never met Krinke personally before they sent him after the ordinary-looking cuss, and you'd be surprised how men lie when a lawman asks them for I.D."

Purvis shrugged and said, "When you meet Von Thaldorf, you won't think him a stupid man. He'd surely know a fellow Austrian if he met one, wouldn't he?"

Longarm shook his head. "Likely not as quick as you or I might, Doc. It's a funny thing, but *I'd* have a tougher time detecting an American speaking Spanish with an American accent than any *Mex* would. An Austrian, speaking English, don't *hear* the mistakes he makes, or he wouldn't *make* 'em. Do you follow my drift?"

Purvis smiled thinly. "Now that you point out the obvious. But you're still barking up the wrong tree. This party was organized back in Omaha, long before either the colonel or the man you're both hunting was in our country. Most of us are native-born midwesterners. I knew some of the family heads long before I decided the future looked more promising in Oregon than Ohio, so—"

"So tell me about the ones as *ain't* native-born Americans," Longarm cut in.

Purvis looked disgusted and said, "Now you're just being silly. The McBrides are Irish Catholics. Sean McBride is short and dark as any Italian. The Hansens are Scandinavian. And, before you point out that a Scandinavian accent sounds Germanic, I'd better point out that Gus Hansen stands six-foot-six in his stocking feet. Von Thaldorf thinks Krinke must have ridden on to Fort Bidwell alone."

Longarm shrugged. "He surely must have rid *some-place,* as he ain't in Rosebud Wash or here."

He shoved his saddles and gear under the nearest wagon and led the mules to the nearest gap to turn them out to graze with the other stock. They had just moved off, slowly because of the heat, when a gent dressed in new and yet-to-be-laundered blue denim marched at him and Purvis, stiff-spined and faster than anyone needed to march on such a hot day. Longarm didn't really need Purvis to tell him who it had to be. But he introduced them to one another, anyway, and Herr Oberst Von Thaldorf actually clicked his booted heels together as he said, "So we meet at last. I have heard of the famous Longarm. At the moment I am still concerned about the Red Indians that *other* Americaner warned us about. I have yet to shoot a Red Indian. Are you certain they are afraid to attack, Herr Longarm?"

Longarm tried not to look disgusted as he sized up the dapper Austrian. Von Thaldorf was trying to look cow, in his store-bought denims and new white Stetson. The dragoon pistol he packed in a military holster looked serious enough. But Longarm had never ridden herd with a hand who sported a moustache so horned with wax the gals in Dodge would hesitate to risk kissing him. The overly clean-cut officer's cheeks were shaved smooth as a baby's behind, even this far out on the trail. The left cheek was scarred as if he'd shaved too close with a cavalry saber one morning. Longarm said, "The Ho ain't *afraid* to hit us, Colonel. They just got too much sense. Every time Indians attack a wagon train the army goes after 'em with Hotchkiss guns. So they don't like to do it unless you give 'em a mighty good reason."

Von Thaldorf looked disappointed. "So? I was hoping for some sport on the trail. What do you think our chances are on buffalo, Herr Longarm?"

"Not good this far west. In the more sensible desert, up around Fort Bidwell, you may spot some pronghorn. Don't shoot at 'em, though. They run so far before they drop that the stringy meat ain't worth it, even in the winter, when it ain't as wormy."

"I do not shoot game for *meat*, Herr Longarm. I am a sportsman, not a butcher."

"I figured you might be, Colonel. By the way, do either of you know who took that shot at me as I was coming in just now?"

Purvis shook his head. Von Thaldorf looked annoyed and said, "At that range, I could not have *missed*. But anyone could see you were a white man. The shot was from my left fired. That is all I know. I did not see who the idiot was, but I was one of those who called out for him to stop."

Longarm thanked him and said, "Well, you gents had best scout up some shade. *I* mean to, as soon as I run an inspection and have a word at each wagon with the others. Whoever fired on me missed, and ain't likely to own up to it now. But I got to make sure everyone understands the orders I just gave on getting through the day."

He moved back inside the wagon ring ahead of them and didn't look back as they did whatever they had a mind to about the hot sun. Longarm resisted the temptation to take off his coat as the sun beat him across the upper back and shoulders.

He banged first on the front wheel of the wagon he had his gear shaded under. A pretty gal stuck her head out the front of the hood, holding the canvas closed from there on down to keep him from seeing if she was dressed or otherwise. He said, "Ma'am, I got some stuff under your wagon bed, and I mean to unroll my bedding there as well in a spell. So please don't move your wagon or leak nothing through the floor boards without fair warning."

She dimpled. "Heavens, you can come inside with us if you like. We've more than enough room," she told him.

Before he could ask who "us" might be, another pretty head popped out to ask the first one who she felt so free to invite under the canvas with them. Then she saw Longarm and added, "Oh, sure, we got *plenty* of room in here."

The first one explained, "We're the Grover girls, on our way to Oregon to plant apples and mayhaps find good husbands in the end."

He grinned up at them. "I'm sure you will, ladies. But ain't it unusual for two young gals to travel so complicated *alone*, no offense?"

The second sister said, "Not really. We were working in Ohio, waiting tables for good tips, when the folks who'd bought this outfit changed their minds at the last moment and offered us a bargain. Driving a covered wagon ain't half as hard as waiting tables, once you set your mind to it."

He said he could see they were strong-willed gals,

85

and moved on to see what else he had to worry about. He had plenty, by the time he had circled the whole ring. There were, as Bull Culhane had said, close enough, a baker's dozen of thirteen emigrant wagons, along with a lighter canopied buckboard and chuck wagon Bradford had dragged along. Half had kids and half the kids were sick or at least fretful from the heat. He made sure every wagon outfit had more than a day's water on hand, including water for the stock, come sundown. He warned them all that, after a day on open salt-bush range, the oxen and riding stock would need plenty of water to start, and at least two good drinks during the night, if anyone meant to make the next sweetwater by daybreak. More than one greenhorn asked who came first if the water ran low. Longarm gave them all the same answer. A thirsty human, riding, would get there, feeling good or not. Nobody would get very far if the critters had to lie down.

Von Thaldorf turned out to be a boarder in the Purvis wagon when it was stopped, riding the trail aboard the mule he'd bought in Rosebud Wash. The doc and his middle-aged but handsome wife had no kids with them. Longarm was too polite to inquire further about sleeping arrangements in one prairie schooner. They figured to get a mite more awkward, now that everyone would be bedded down in broad day.

The bearded Silas Bradford had managed to avoid Longarm for a time, no doubt with some effort. But as Longarm moved back toward the Grover wagon the erstwhile wagonmaster popped out from between two others and announced, "I'd like a word with you alone,

Longarm. You should have told me who you was right off. It could have avoided us some mutual crawfishing."

"I don't recall crawfishing, old son. But if you're asking if we're straight, we are, as long as you don't act silly no more. Why have you been greening these greenhorns so? Are you planning on starting your own Wild West show some day, or are you just mean-hearted?"

"Don't rawhide me, damn it. No gals are looking. I was serious about them Indians, Longarm. I don't know how you rode through 'em alone like you done, but I do know they're *out* there, damn it."

Longarm said, "I know that, too. I just ate breakfast with 'em. They ain't hostiles. They've been scouting you-all because we make them as nervous as they make us. Hell, Bradford, *you* ought to know they're harmless, the way you and your brother have been running the mail through 'em along this very trail for a coon's age."

Bradford looked away. "It's different, riding alone on a good mount with a good repeating rifle. I ain't as used to herding slowpokes offering such a tempting target. I know they *say* the Diggers in these parts ain't on the warpath. But tell that to the old Digger who gave this trail its very name. *He* sure as hell met at least one heap bad Injun out here, and he wasn't even wearing boots worth stealing."

Longarm shrugged and said, "We're talking about ancient history in a time of trouble. The only band in these parts, now, just assured me they wasn't looking for trouble. I know some Indians fib. But I *was* wearing boots when they had me cold last night. So I'm tempted to buy their tale."

He fished out two smokes, offered one to Bradford, and lit it for him. "Whatever happened, long ago or recent, you did get 'em this far alive, if somewhat poorer, and we'll be at least fifteen miles farther come sunrise. Meanwhile, you'd best bed down somewhere. I ain't as dumb as you, but I mean to drive this outfit, some, once it's safe to do so."

Bradford protested, "There you go rawhiding me again, damn it. I ain't *used* to being rawhided, Longarm."

"Don't act dumb and nobody will have to, then. I just told you we was straight, not that I'm impressed by that '74. By the way, you really ought to get a proper holster for that thumb buster, Silas. It's dangerous as hell to pack a gun with its muzzle so close to your own balls."

"You'd be surprised how quick I can draw with her riding like so, Longarm."

"Please don't show me. Most of the kiddies is napping, and the ground all about is too hard to offer you a proper burial."

Bradford swore under his breath and turned away. Longarm shrugged and moved closer to the wagon. As he hunkered down to unroll his bedding in the miserly shade, one of the Grover girls hissed at him and whispered, "Get up here, you silly! Do you want to die in your sleep?"

He straightened up to ask, "You heard, ma'am?"

"Of course we did," she replied. "They told us in Rye Patch both Bradford brothers are notorious gunslicks, and you just shamed Silas awful! How could you even consider going to sleep in the open, when his wagon cover can't be fifty feet away?"

He started to tell her Silas Bradford didn't look up to cold-blooded murder in broad day. But that could have been a dumb thing to say. So he said, "Well, if you insist," and tossed his bedding up to her.

She caught it with a bare arm and hauled it inside. When Longarm followed he found both sisters wearing nothing but their shifts and reclining on their own silk quilts, atop their provisions.

From inside, the white canvas cast a soft tan light over everything. The half-dressed gals looked more rosy than tan. They were likely feeling the heat. He knew *he* was. He said, "This sure is hospitable, ladies. I hope you won't take it wrong if I make some other suggestions on keeping comfortable in the desert."

The one who said to call her Doris asked what he had in mind, blushing redder. The sister called Tess elbowed her and said to let him just say what he wanted. He gulped. "You may have noticed how hot it is, and it figures to get hotter before it gets cooler," he said. "The best way to beat the heat in bed is stripped down entirely, atop the bedding. I'll trust you not to peek if you'll trust me, and if we hang my tarp up in the middle . . ."

Then he stopped and added, "Don't you want to wait till I do, Miss Tess?" as the older and no-doubt worldlier one proceeded to shuck her shift off over her head.

Both Longarm and her younger sister gasped as she tossed the shift aside and lay back stark, asking, "What next?"

Longarm laughed despite himself. "It don't seem so pure shocking when Indians do that, ma'am. But it's good to see you has a practical approach to desert living. I'll just haul my gear and me farther back and do the same, now."

Tess sat up on one elbow to ask, "How come? Are you bashful?"

Her sister protested. "You're teasing the poor man spiteful, you mean thing!"

Tess said, "No I ain't. I ain't had a man since Ohio, and I guess I know who's feeling teased right now."

Longarm saw that neither one had any intention of making room for him to get by. He tossed his hat past them instead and began to unbutton his duds as he said, "Well, I was raised never to argue with my hostess, and the last lady I spent the day with, naked, was off limits, so . . ."

Doris gasped, "Have you both gone crazy? Do you expect me to take part in some kind of Roman orgy?"

Tess said, "When in Rome, be a good sport. Or crawl in the back if you don't want to watch. I might not *be* so hot, right now, if you hadn't stole that good-looking customer from me the night we left Ohio."

Longarm gulped and said, "Hold on, ladies. What was that about a *customer?* I thought it was understood you two was *waitress* gals."

Tess laughed. "We were, and I'm still *waiting,* bashful!"

He got out of his duds. Doris said they were both just horrid and crawled out of sight over the pile of provisions. Longarm tried not to look wistfully at her sweet little rump as she hauled it out of view. For Tess was reclining with her thighs apart in welcome, now.

He rolled aboard and she moaned as he entered her. He liked the way *she* felt down there, too, but asked her to keep it down to a roar as he moved it in her sneaky, all too aware how close the other wagons were, and how voices carried through canvas.

Thanks to the way he'd saved his own life in the all-day company of a not-bad naked Indian lady the day before, Longarm was horny enough despite the heat. The air was dry enough to drink up sweat as fast as it beaded, so sweating in desert air actually had a cooling effect.

Tess rolled her head back and forth as she gasped, "Yes, yes, that's the way I like it and that's just the way I've been *needing* it! Oh, Doris, you don't know what you're missing!"

From the darker rear of the wagon, the other sister sobbed, "Shut up, damn it. Can't you just *do* it? Do you have to *brag* about it, too?"

Longarm felt she was showing off, too, even though it felt just grand. But when they were finished, he noticed that Doris lay on her stomach, watching. He rolled over on his back, muttering, "Why, thank you, Lord. That was a nicer surprise than anything this side of a pay raise could have been."

Then he felt a naked woman atop him, somehow cooler, and opened his eyes to see it was Doris, demanding her turn. That was no chore, since he was still hard, and she proceeded to do all the work with her younger and shapelier body. He hauled her pretty face down to kiss it and feel her firm breasts against his bare chest. Tess rolled over, propped herself on one elbow, and muttered, "Hey, I thought you didn't approve of Roman notions, Sis."

Doris moaned, "I don't. What we're doing is sinful and I just know we'll all wind up in hell, some day. But this ain't the day to worry about that."

So they had a Roman orgy until it got too hot. Then they all slept until the sun got more orange through the canvas, late that afternoon, and had another one. For once Doris got over her first shyness, she was even bolder and more inclined to experiments than her earthier sister.

Chapter 6

Everyone else in the party seemed pleased they had met up with Longarm by the time he called the first trail break after dark. As Longarm was watering his own mules Dr. Purvis caught up with him to say, "I can't believe how far we've traveled since sundown, and it's so much *easier!* I was an idiot to have hired that Bradford ruffian!"

"Just a mite inexperienced, Doc," Longarm said, "Old Silas might have been right, if this was prairie and them Ho was, say, Pawnee."

"I thought the Pawnee were friendlies, Longarm."

"That's what I mean, inexperienced. Lakota and Cheyenne only hit you when they're pissed off and on

93

the warpath. Pawnee admire white notions so much that they seldom miss a chance to rob an easy target. I mind one time when the Cheyenne had risen and I was scouting for the army, along with some Pawnee. They scouted just fine. Pawnee hate Cheyenne. We still had to hang a couple for looting an isolated homestead they came across as they was searching for Dull Knife's camp. But let's forget Indian troubles this summer. We got enough to worry about. Like, right now, my back teeth is floating and if I don't take a leak now, Lord knows how I'll hold out till the *next* trail break."

He excused himself to walk away from the trail into the waist-high salt bush until he was hidden enough by darkness to relieve himself. He was just about to rise when he heard someone coming and, not wanting to explain the obvious, stayed put.

It was the Austrian officer and old Doc Purvis's wife, Martha. It wasn't too clear why the lady felt the need of an escort on the way to a squat in the salt bush, at first. Then they both dropped out of sight and, from the sounds they made, Longarm knew they sure weren't *shitting* over that way. She was moaning that he was killing her and he kept telling her she was his little "Leap Thing." Doris had been right; other folk screwing sure seemed silly. Longarm knew that if he got up now they'd feel even sillier. So he just stayed put, like the tar baby, till she moaned, "Oh, I could go on like this forever, Wolfgang. But we'd best get back before someone notices we're not there."

That was the only sensible thing she'd said, in Longarm's opinion, since the colonel had thrown her down in the weeds.

Von Thaldorf must have thought so, too. A few minutes later he helped her up and they moved off, looking innocent.

Longarm grimaced and got to his own feet, buckling up, as he muttered half aloud, "Well, he may be an officer, but he ain't no gentleman, as I defines the same. A real gent don't mess with another gent's silverware, servants, or wedded wife. You'd think they'd teach such things at fancy universities."

He moved back to the trail, untethered his mule from the Hansen wagon he'd found handiest, and called, "All right, let's move 'em *out!* Stay on the trail and hold your pace and position. I'm riding ahead to scout some!"

He did so, leaving the pack mule behind. He had no sooner cleared Bradford's lead team when he heard hoofbeats behind him and turned to see Von Thaldorf overtaking him in the moonlight. As the Austrian fell in beside him, he asked Longarm where they were going.

"Indians told me there's a poison water hole ahead," Longarm said. "I want to position it exactly, so we can lead the stock around it upwind. Stock on short water rations ain't got much sense when they smell *any* kind of water."

Von Thaldorf asked, "How much brine could even a dumb brute drink before it gagged? I have been salting my food all my life and I've never yet overdone it enough to kill myself."

"I ain't talking about plain old table salt, bad as that would be on thirsty innards," Longarm said. "Some desert sinks is real chemistry sets. You name anything as will mix with water and you're likely to find a puddle of it out here somewhere."

As they rode on, he continued, "The Indians say stock poisoned up ahead die sudden, strung out along

95

the trail. They failed to mention any settlers doing the same. That reads like something sneaky, mixed thin in what tastes tolerable. It hit the well-watered stock as they dried out some, sweating and pulling the wagons. The humans likely just got to feeling puny. Mayhaps suffered a bad case of the trots before they got to the better water farther on."

Von Thaldorf shrugged. *"If* those Red Indians were telling you the *truth,* of course. What if they just made up the story to keep us from using the water hole?"

Longarm thought before he decided, "Mighty complicated slickery, even for a white man. Why warn us about one water hole and announce there's another one, a good one, less than eight hours farther?"

"What if the nearest water is good and the one they directed you to is the poison one?"

"I wish you hadn't said that. I know Indians brag on not fibbing as much as we do, but *that's* a big fib, too. Every honor code makes a point of telling the truth, and lots of folk still lie."

They rode on some more before he decided, "Too complicated. They had me cold if they'd wanted to harm a white man easy. Indians lie at least as smart as white men, but it's true they seldom lie just for the hell of it."

"Would not that scout, Bradford, know? He's ridden this trail many times, *nicht wahr?"*

"Yeah, and I'd still trust nine out of ten Indians first. Let's see how easy it is to get around the suspicious water before we ride back and ask him. It ain't like the others are hot on our heels."

He loped his mule forward, the Austrian followed, riding well, and less than an hour later Longarm reined in as he spotted moonlit water ahead. The pool looked like a water-filled shell crater left over from some mysterious desert war. As they dismounted Longarm said, "Hell, it's hand-dug, all right, but the winds has blown most of the spoil away. So there's no way to fill her in again even if we wanted to."

He hunkered down, digging his heels into the steep slope to keep from taking a moonlight swim in his duds, and dipped a finger in the water. Von Thaldorf stared around. "Would not there be animal remains here if the water was really dangerous?" he asked.

Longarm said, "Wouldn't mean much if you *did* spy bones near water. Coyotes like to wash their meals down."

He sniffed at his wet finger. "I thought them Ho was decent folk. Wild garlic is more rare than skeletons around desert water holes. So it has to be arsenic chloride. If I was willing to taste it, it'd taste sort of sweet, too. I'll take my nose's word it's arsenic, though."

As he stood up, Von Thaldorf was bending over. The Austrian picked up a sharpened wooden stake he had found in the weeds. "This looks as if it had been driven into the earth and then pulled out," he said.

Longarm took the length of wood from him, held it up to the moonbeams, and growled, "Rusty nail holes at the blunt end, too. What we have here is a case of attempted murder."

The other lawman looked blank. Longarm explained, "This is what's left of a posted sign. Somebody decent went to considerable trouble to warn other pilgrims, after he wondered about wild garlic, too. It was likely some prospector. They're better at chemistry than most."

Von Thaldorf gasped and said, *"Herr Gott!* You mean some fiend destroyed the warning deliberately?"

Longarm raised the sharp end to his face. "This sign-post didn't pull *itself* out of the hard-baked dirt," he growled. "Smells like it was done this side of spring. The wood as was underground ain't never been rained on since."

Von Thaldorf nodded, but said, "We shall have to narrow it down better than that, before we can bring the villain to justice."

Longarm tossed the stake away. "We might ask Hans Krinke about it, if and when," he remarked.

"I don't understand, Longarm. I agree Krinke is a criminal, but could he be the *only* criminal in your Wild West?"

"Longarm chuckled. "That'd be too much to hope for. But if it wasn't him, how could he have known this was poison water?"

Von Thaldorf started to say something dumb. Then he nodded grimly and said, "Of course. He is, as you call me, a greenhorn, and one tends to doubt he speaks to local Indians very often."

"Now you're reading sign, old son," Longarm said. "Whoever destroyed the warning was warned by it not to drink the water. So he never. Then, just in case some-one might be following him close, he wanted to give them a chance to poison themselves instead."

Longarm kicked some dirt in the pond, cursed softly, and added, "We'd best ride on back. I'll whip up a cross of scrap wood and cut over here to post this hole again as we steer the others by."

"A cross?" Von Thaldorf asked as they mounted up.

"Would *you* trust water if you saw what looked like a

grave marker beside it?" Longarm asked. "Lots of folk can't read, and a simple cross saves tedious lettering that would only fade in the sun, anyway."

Back at the wagons, Silas Bradford said of course he knew about the poison water ahead and hadn't intended to stop there in the first place. Longarm asked about the missing sign and Bradford said, "I wouldn't know. Like you said afore I got a chance to, it's a good notion to steer well clear of the place aboard a thirsty mount. I told you I generally rides this trail alone, at night. I'll bet them Diggers done it."

Longarm did not argue. He reined in to let the lead wagons move up the trail ahead, for now. But before he could join the Grover girls for some more amusing conversation he noticed Von Thaldorf was still sticking to him like an infernal tick. He knew either of the Grovers would no doubt welcome an addition to their next party, and it sure might make life safer for the colonel if he found a gal who wasn't wed to play around with. But Longarm had never acted the part of a pimp before and he wasn't about to start now, even if it busted his back. So he asked Von Thaldorf what else he could do for him.

The Austrian kept his voice low, as if he thought the folk in the passing wagons cared. "I have been thinking about our mutual friend, Herr Krinke," he said.

Longarm said, "He ain't our mutual nothing. He's your prisoner, if we ever overtake him. But, while we're on the subject, do you have a photograph or at least a decent description of the rascal? I don't even know for sure what color eyes he has. No offense, but your copper badges in Vienna town sure book prisoners sloppy."

"I have his dossier, if you would like to read it over," Von Thaldorf said. "I have no photograph and he was never, as you say, booked. He got word there was a warrant for his arrest and, as you Wild Westers say, lit out before the police arrived."

"Then how in thunder do *you* mean to spot him in a crowd, Colonel?"

Von Thaldorf patted his holstered dragoon pistol thoughtfully as he explained, "I was assigned to his case because, working under cover, I had attended subversive meetings *he* attended. I confess I am not certain of the color of his eyes. It is hard to judge such things in a smoky beer cellar. But I know his face, and I know his voice. Your young Herr Krinke is given to making speeches swine should never make about their betters."

That gave Longarm an opening too good to miss. He didn't have to risk Herta's hometown reputation at all. "I *heard* he was mixed up with the socialist movement. Is that why we're out to arrest him?"

The Austrian lawman shrugged. "Preaching the wisdom of an atheist named Marx in a Catholic absolute monarchy is not polite. But, as we have explained to your idealistic State Department, the man is more than a simple revolutionary. To finance his own radical cell, he also printed Austrian bank notes, forged passports, and even honorable discharges from the Austro–Hungarian Army!"

Longarm chuckled. "I'll bet *that* made 'em mad as hell. We have a hell of a time keeping *our* troops from straying, and *we* allow them to bend their backbones now and again. I forget who mentioned it, back in

Denver, I reckon, but wasn't one of your own princes mixed up with old Hans and his red notions?"

Von Thaldorf snapped, "Those charges have been dropped. Crown Prince Rudolf is an emotional youth who allowed himself to be taken advantage of."

"Do tell? What did he get mixed up in? Something dirty, like drinking beer with common folk?"

The Austrian shrugged. *Ach,* would it was so simple as whoring and getting drunk. I fear Prince Rudolf will come to a bad end, no matter how we watch out for him. There are limits, after all, to what even our police can do about a headstrong teenager who will some day be emperor."

"You just get to arrest his friends, huh?"

Von Thaldorf didn't understand the sarcasm. *"Ach,* if only one could. Krinke and his group, as I said, are known subversives with criminal records. Lately, Prince Rudolf has taken to inviting Ungers to his private hunting lodge at Mayerling, where they drink tokay and listen all night to sad gypsy music, we hope. The servants are loyal to His Highness, so it does not count when they say nothing but Unger orgies are taking place at Mayerling."

Longarm said, "I give up. What in thunder is an Unger?"

"Is it not obvious? You English speakers simply put an 'H' on it. Unger is the German for Hungarian. I told you Prince Rudolf is an Austro–Hungarian crown prince, *nicht wahr?"*

"I thought it was *Magyar.* Damned if I recalls where I heard that."

Von Thaldorf reached in one of his saddlebags as he explained. "Magyar is what Ungers call themselves in

101

their own strange tongue. We can't be bothered with a primitive language related to Turkish. Here, let me give you my dossier on Krinke. I have memorized it by heart, and you should not be confused about side issues. We are hunting an Austrian counterfeiter, not crown princes or Hungarian gypsies!"

Longarm took the manila envelope but said he would read it sometime when the light was better. He put it in his own saddlebag. He did not say he still had reservations about the charges against Krinke.

Still, Von Thaldorf said, "You know, now, Krinke is a *killer* as well as a common criminal."

Longarm shrugged. "I know whoever pulled that stake out of the ground ahead would like to kill folk. I know Krinke makes a grand suspect, since he wasn't stretched out poisoned by a pool he should have took for sweetwater, otherwise. But let's not leap into that can of worms just yet, pard. There's other ways it could work. We still don't know for sure that your man preceded us up this trail."

Von Thaldorf snapped, "He *has* to be ahead of us. He could not have evaded us both back in Rosebud Wash."

Longarm nodded grudgingly. "They noticed you. They noticed *me*. But it's a funny thing, Colonel. I couldn't find anyone who noticed *Krinke*, back there."

"What do you mean? Why should they have taken serious note of a total stranger during the confusion of this wagon train's arrival and departure?"

"I already said, Colonel. Like yourself, I assumed Krinke could have mixed in with these other pilgrims and left town with this party. But I don't see him around here, do you?"

"Of course not. He left alone."

"Do tell? When? I know for a fact he wasn't left behind after the rest of you lit out. That means he *should* have left ahead, like you keep saying. But how come nobody *saw* him? And on what? They knew in town that you hired a mule. They knew in town that I hired two. But nobody recalls hiring a big dog or a billy goat to anyone before this wagon train left town, and Fort Bidwell's sure a long walk."

The Austrian thought for a moment, then suggested, "Could he not have stolen a mount, Longarm?"

"In a town that small, without it being reported to Bull Culhane? If you ever mean to occasion gossip in a bitty trail town, Colonel, don't hire a mount, just *steal* one. I've seen a posse of het-up townees ride fifty miles in a night after a horse thief. If Krinke had left Rosebud Wash aboard a stolen mount, we'd have heard about it by now."

Von Thaldorf said, "I have heard your Wild Wester views on horse thieves. But Herr Bradford pointed out another trail just beyond the first spring we stopped at. What if our Hansel took the other route to Fort Bidwell?"

"We'd have still heard about it. The posse would have taken this one. Mounted or not, Krinke would be mighty dumb to follow a trail he'd been warned was a dead end to disaster, wouldn't he?"

"*If* he'd been warned, you mean. He is, like me, a greenhorn. Could he not have taken the other trail by mistake?"

Longarm shrugged. "If he did, that lets him off as our signpost puller, but it makes him mighty green indeed. To follow any trail a man needs directions, starting out. I failed to find anyone in town who advised me

103

to take the Salty Trail. Nobody knows for sure it goes anywhere, let alone Fort Bidwell."

"Ah, but what if our clever Hans plans on going somewhere else?"

"Already considered that. There's only two places a man could aim for out here. He could make for Fort Bidwell and greener pastures, or he could double back through Rosebud Wash to Rye Patch, after leading us on a snipe hunt."

"You also hunt *snipe* out here in this desert, Longarm?"

Longarm sighed and said, "All too often, when the gent I'm chasing is slick. The farther we chase Krinke across this dust bowl, the more I can't help wondering if he ain't sitting in the Palace Hotel in San Francisco right now, drinking Anchor beer and feeling mighty pleased with himself. The Transcontinental Flyer takes you there from Rye Patch in no time, you know. And what in thunder would either a born rabble-rouser or a professional criminal want in Oregon? Your boy is a city slicker, not a logger or a farmer, Colonel."

Von Thaldorf told him Krinke had to be somewhere out ahead of them. Then he showed he had done some fox hunting, too, in his time, by moaning, *"Herr Gott,* if he simply took that other trail a few miles, camped until we passed, and doubled back . . . But how can we be *sure,* Longarm?"

Longarm said, "We can't. Not before we get to Fort Bidwell, and I ain't about to strand these emigrants in the desert in any case. If he makes Fort Bidwell ahead of us, the army will be able to tell us. They don't get all that many visitors at a desert post in high summer. Any kind of white man riding in alone across the alkali flats

104

attracts a certain amount of attention. So it won't matter if he's disguised and telling fibs. If he has been through, in recent memory, we can likely get the army to help us ride him down. They ain't got much else to do, and there's no way in hell anyone could get far with separate patrols beelining for every known water hole, so—"

"What if he is *not* ahead of us?" the other lawman cut in bleakly. "What if he doubled back and is, as you say, laughing at us?"

Longarm shrugged. "I reckon we'll just have to go all the way back to the railroad tracks and start from scratch, Colonel. I don't like to be laughed at much. Do you?"

Chapter 7

Longarm had led the Purvis party to the safer water the friendly Ho had told him of by the time dawn threatened. The salt bush had given way to more sage, so he didn't have to take the Indians' word for the glorified mud puddle. Sage wouldn't grow with its roots too salty. Before he let them set up camp he assembled the family heads and warned them, "I mean to leave this campsite no unhealthier than we found it. That means all the trash that won't burn in one pile, and nobody shitting within two hundred yards of the trail. Eat light and go easy on the coffee for breakfast. Don't give the kids *any*. It's hard to keep a wide-awake kid bedded down through the hot hours. Come nightfall, we'll of course eat more and coffee hard. Are there any questions?"

Purvis asked how far they had to go. "We're better than half way to half ways," Longarm said. Then he turned to Bradford and said, "You'd know better than me about the next water, Silas."

The bearded man shrugged. "A good night's ride. I make her about thirty, forty miles."

Longarm swore under his breath. "All right, that means the next day camp will be dry. So get your folk as well as your livestock to swill all the water they can today, and make sure you pack plenty along. Fill open buckets as well, and drink that water first."

The tall blond Hansen cleared his throat and asked if it wouldn't be easier on them in the long run if they tried to make the next water in one forced march. Longarm shook his head and said, "That ain't the way you keep oxen pulling. Keep 'em watered and they'll give you fifteen, maybe twenty miles a day, day after day. Drive 'em harder than that and, watered or not, they'll just lay down and die on you. It's the only way they have of protesting cruel working conditions."

"Damn it, my wife can walk thirty miles in one night if she has to," Hansen said.

Longarm nodded but asked, "Can she pull your wagon?"

Some of the others laughed.

Longarm laughed, too, and told Hansen, "She don't have to walk at all, unless she'd like to stretch her legs from time to time. This ain't an athletic contest, pard. Getting there can be half the fun, if you don't overdo it."

There was no further argument. As the meeting

broke up, Longarm did his own chores, hauling some water to the Grover wagon as well, so by the time he climbed up in the wagon with the two bawdy sisters the sun was up and they were both in need, they said, of other services. But the second hot day spent with the two little gals wasn't half as much fun.

Fortunately, Tess said she was too tired at the next camp, the dry and really uncomfortable one, and when they got to water and even some cottonwood shade at the next one, Doris was the one who said she just had to get some sleep. He suspected they had planned it that way on the trail at night, behind his back. He didn't care. It made for less effort, and the loving was nicer now, no matter which one he was loving up.

Longarm only caught the colonel and Martha Purvis one more time, almost tripping over them in the sage during a nighttime trail break. The moon was starting to quarter darker now, so they never noticed him. He had sort of hoped the colonel would find someone else, before Doc Purvis caught them at it. There was no way Longarm could ask the colonel not to screw another man's wife without risking a mighty noisy argument, so he didn't. He didn't know why this should make him want to avoid the eyes of old Doc Purvis, but it did. The Doc was a nice old gent, and anyone could see he was fond of his woman. Around the fire at mealtimes Martha Purvis smiled to herself a lot. She was likely feeling prettier, these days, than she had for some time.

But the real trouble came from outside the party, on the dawn of a day that should have been nicer. They were in a valley between two close-set ranges, where the higher elevation let taller brush and even some cottonwood clumps survive, and as Bradford had promised, there was a willow-circled all-year pool where he'd said it would be. But after that it was all downhill.

Longarm, Von Thaldorf, and Bradford rode on ahead when they spotted wood smoke rising above the pond-side willows. As they approached the only water within forty miles a quartet of shabby white gents stepped into view between them and the water, all four wearing guns.

As Longarm greeted them, one called out, "That's close enough, pilgrim. If you want water, we got business to discuss. For we welcome you to Turner's Spring. I'm Jake Turner, proprietor, and water is two bits a gallon or a dollar a keg. We ain't greedy."

Longarm said, "Yes, you are. This is a public right-of-way on federal land, friend."

Turner spat. "Don't try to fool me with law talk, boy," he said. "I knows my law. The government allows first-comers to stake mineral claims on unexplored federal land, and water is a mineral, since it can't be animal or vegetable, right?"

Longarm shook his head. "Water rights and mineral rights don't come under the same federal statutes. Even if they did, your claim won't wash. You can't claim first discovery on a trail that's already been mapped and, hell, used to carry the U. S. Mail!"

Turner shrugged. "I don't see no post office around here, pilgrim. There ain't *nothin'* within a hard day's ride of this water. That's on account of it's the only water there *is,* and it's *mine!*"

Longarm said, "I ain't saying you boys can't have all the water you want, Turner. The folk with me has the same rights to it, no more, no less. Before this discussion gets any sillier, I'd best inform you I'm the law.

That's how come I know so much about federal water regulations, see?"

Turner shook his head. "I don't care if you're the Queen of Sheba, boy. There ain't no law courts around here, neither. As the elected mayor of Turner Township as well as sole proprietor of Turner's Spring, I has lawsomely appointed these boys with me the police force of our fair city. So stick *that* in your pipe and smoke it."

At Longarm's left, Von Thaldorf murmured, "Whenever you say, Longarm."

Bradford, on his right, called out, "You boys are making an awesome mistake. Both these gents is law, and I am Silas Bradford of Rye Patch. You've heard of me and my brother, Caleb, of course?"

Turner laughed. "Not much. In case you're wondering what makes me so brave this morning, I got more of my peace officers covering from the trees ahint us. But, hell, why are we all talking so tough? Two bits a gallon makes more sense than a gunfight, don't it?"

Bradford murmured, "The old Doc has lots of money, and there's another water hole closer than he says to the north. We only needs enough for the stock."

Longarm shook his head. "The party I'm leading means to water and camp for the day here, on Uncle Sam," he told Turner. "That's me. I'm willing to forget you just tried to commit the considerable crime of extortion on federal land if you're willing to stop talking dumb. You are right about law courts being in short supply in these parts. So now I'm riding into them trees to secure that water and I'll kill any man as makes one move to stop me."

It might have worked out had not Von Thaldorf drawn his big dragoons as Longarm heeled his own

111

mule forward. But the four of them took the colonel's move as an invitation to slap leather, and did. So the next few moments got noisy as hell.

Longarm yelled, "Hold on, God damn it!" even as someone put a bullet in his mount, and might have put one in him as well, had not he been spilled. He drew his own .44 as he went down sideways and rolled clear of the flailing mule. He heard the colonel's big dragoon go off behind him but didn't look back. He spied a more important target in the gunsmoke haze the other way and shot the fool firing at him with both guns before he could work up the sense to take aim.

As the trail bully went down, a rifle ball took Longarm's hat for a short morning ride. "Oh, shit!" he muttered, as he crabbed sideways to get behind his downed mule, now that someone was making good on Turner's threat from the treeline.

He had just taken cover when he heard a string of rapid-fire shots among the trees, from what sounded like the same repeating rifle. Then it got very quiet.

Longarm glanced over his shoulder. Von Thaldorf was dismounted, smoking gun in hand. Both the colonel's mule and Silas Bradford were vanishing back down the trail in the considerable dust.

The Austrian asked, "See anything?"

"No," Longarm snapped. Get *down* here with me, you asshole!"

Then he turned to look over the top. The gunsmoke was clearing and four figures lay stretched on the ground in various conditions of sudden death. Von Thaldorf hunkered down beside him and seemed jovial, considering, as he said, "I got at least two of them, I am

112

sure. We both fired at their leader. So we share him, *ja?*"

"I don't care if you want him all, to stuff. We might have avoided the whole infernal fight, *my* way."

"Perhaps. Perhaps not. Now the matter is settled once and for all, *nicht wahr?*"

"Keep down before you get your *wahr* nixed by them rascals in the trees! I sure hope Bradford thinks to mention all this as he tears by the others. For we're pinned in the open, good!"

As if to prove his point, they heard another rifle shot from the willows. The shot didn't seem to be aimed their way. Then a voice called out, "Hold your fire, gents. I'm on your side, coming out."

They did, and a bearded gent in a red shirt came out of the trees aboard a big black mule, a Spencer repeater across his saddle bows. He looked so much like the vamoosed Silas Bradford that Longarm wasn't at all surprised when he called out, "I'm the U. S. Mail, in the person of Caleb Bradford. Wasn't that my baby brother I just noticed getting menaced with you all?"

Longarm rose, reloading, as he said it sure had been. "What was all that shooting about just now? In the trees, I mean."

The older and obviously braver Bradford brother spat. "There was six more camped by the water with their ponies. Had to shoot a pony as got caught in the crossfire as well. I was watching with amusement from that ridge, yonder, till it got light enough to get the picture and slide down the scree ahint 'em. What was they, water hogs?"

113

Longarm nodded. "They were trying to be. What's the story farther north, Caleb?" he went on.

"Ain't none. Ought to be clear sailing all the way up to Fort Bidwell, now. I just rid down from there with their letters home. Got 'em aboard my mule, here."

Before Longarm could get around to less important matters than the trail ahead, Von Thaldorf asked Bradford about Hans Krinke. The mail rider shrugged and said, "I wouldn't know. I just rid in, dropped off the mail, picked up another pouch, and headed back. You'll see why, once you get there. It's a shitty post, even for the army."

The three of them turned as they heard hoofbeats. Purvis, the other Bradford brother, and half the men in the party came up the trail all at once. As they reined in, Longarm yelled, "That was no doubt fun. Now most of you had best ride back, and don't never do that again. When you hear shots you're supposed to guard your families, not charge blind."

"It's all right," Silas Bradford yelled back. "I told 'em to come along and back my play. Hey, what are *you* doing here, Caleb?"

The older brother laughed. "Beat you to the rescue again, baby brother. Tell you all about it as we breaks fast. For I may as well spend the day here with you, now that the sun's riz."

Within an hour they had the bodies out of the way and the camp set up. It was so nice among the trees that both Grover girls insisted on getting laid before the day was over.

Longarm found it ever harder to maintain a sensible pace as the monotonous journey wore on. The emigrants

114

knew they were more than three-quarters of the way to Fort Bidwell and, by another Basin and Range paradox, the water holes got closer together even as the country got more ferocious.

One morning as he called a halt by a mud hole on an otherwise featureless, bare playa, Longarm called the leaders together and said, "It's time we had this out, gents. For openers, I'd best tell you something the history books and Nat Buntline's Wild West magazines skim over. This is your first overland wagon trip and, if you've a lick of sense, it'll be your last."

There was a chuckle of agreement from the otherwise sullen crowd. "Everyone pictures the wagon years the way they never happened," Longarm said. "Forget them lithographs of circled wagons surrounded by savage Sioux on the lone prairie. That hardly ever happened, and it's hard as hell to die on range rich enough for buffalo. Everybody started out with plenty of supplies, some with more than they needed. They had to abandon so many sides of bacon and sacks of flour before they reached the South Pass that the Indians got fat just watching 'em pass by. The dying times wasn't in the early parts of the passage. The dying came later, after they'd almost *made* it. For by then they *was* low on supplies, and getting anxious enough to take chances, like a short-cut across Death Valley to save a few days, or the Donner party pushing into the Sierras as the first snows were falling because, what the hell, they was almost to California and didn't have enough provisions left to winter this side of that range."

He paused to let that sink in, then went on, "They could have made it through the winter, boring as it sounds, camped among the settlements along the

Truckee. But they took a chance, and you know what happened then."

Some looked as though they did not, so he told them. "They got snowed in. They was close enough to the Great Vale of California to *walk* it, in decent weather. Rescue parties who found 'em in the spring did reach 'em on foot, as a matter of fact. But by then there wasn't much left of the party. Them still alive had made it by eating the first ones to die. But I don't want you to study on their unusual survival rations. I want you to study on what would have happened had they used their heads. They'd made it all the way from the Big Muddy, bright and chipper. Then they got impatient, almost within sound of the California mission bells. So they started pushing too hard."

The Irishman, McArtle, laughed nervously and said, "Well, if there is one thing we don't need to fear, this day, it would be freezing!"

Longarm waited for the laughter to die. Then he nodded. "You can worry about that on the Applegate Trail, once you're out of this desert," he told them. "You'll only be a third of the way to your Oregon homesteads by the time we part at Fort Bidwell, and not even *this* summer can last forever. But, sticking to here and now, the reason the water holes are getting closer together is that the country is getting lower as we approach the High Sierra. Don't ask me why. I wasn't there when the Lord shoved the sierras up and this basin down. The heat ain't going to get less, it's going to get worse. According to that mail rider who stopped with us a few days ago, we ain't on the so-called Siwash Trail any more. From here on up to the fort has been well surveyed and the army uses it when it ain't so infernal hot out here. It's a good thing, too. For there's so-called alkali lakes all about that ain't sure they're lakes all the time. Straying off the trail can get you bogged to the axles in pure kitchen lye. I want folks to stay closer to the trail from here on. It can't be helped. There ain't no fodder for your stock from here on, as you may have noticed. You'll have to feed 'em grain, and if you're low on grain they can get by on baking flour. Just make sure you mix the mash with water before they eat it, lest you bloat 'em. I don't want to hear no more bullshit about twenty-mile nights. The next water is thirty miles. We'll camp mid-way, come sunrise tomorrow."

There was a murmur of protest. Longarm said, "Damn it, that's bullshit, and I said I didn't want to hear it."

"Sure, what if we're midway and the darling sun ain't up?" McArtle insisted. "Wouldn't it make as much sense to go on a few miles?"

Longarm shook his head. "What for? We'd still have to make day camp at the next water. It makes more sense to rest stock cool than to drive 'em a mile farther than they have to move in one night. I know you're all anxious to get this over with. Me and the colonel, here, have even better reasons to want to get to Fort Bidwell fast. But getting there in good shape beats getting there a day sooner, all wore out. You folks still have to push on across more dry country once you rest up and restock at Fort Bidwell. So think of it as an unusually nice rest stop instead of your final goal, and you won't feel so proddy on the trail, hear?"

They said they had been cheered immensely and broke up. The Austrian moved off. Dr. Purvis remained

117

behind. "I'd like a private word with you, Deputy," he said.

Longarm said, "Shoot."

"Someone is sure to, if you don't start using some common sense," Purvis said. "As a doctor, I know the only cure for satyriasis is castration or a bullet in the cranium. But, for God's sake, you *have* those oversexed and unwanted Grover girls to vent your lust on. Can't you leave other men's wives alone?"

Longarm frowned. "Sure I can. I was brought up by the Good Book, Doc. Who says I've been messing with your woman?

Purvis sniffed. "Don't be ridiculous. I know I can trust *my* wife. She was the one who told me about you and Inga Hansen."

Longarm laughed incredulously. "Now, that's funny as well as pure impossible, Doc. I'll allow that big blonde is a handsome woman, but she's married up with a moose who'd make Don Juan think twice, and *he* was a fighting man. Why would your woman want to say such a spiteful thing bout me and old Inga? No offense, but it's pure fiction, without so much as a wink to base it on."

Purvis said, "Look, I'm not making a moral judgment. As captain of this expedition, it's my duty to keep peace between the members of the party. You're not a member of the party. So unless you can behave yourself I'm afraid you'll have to ride on alone."

"No I won't," Longarm said. "We're in dangerous country now. Did Miss Martha tell you direct she saw me and Inga Hansen acting dirty?"

Purvis shook his head and said, "It was reported to her by another member of the party. As wife of the captain, it's Martha's duty to keep an eye on the moral situation. When we were told about you and the Grover girls it was Martha, in fact, who told me it was just as well, since it removed temptation on the trail from many a married man. But Jesus Christ, Longarm! *Inga Hansen?*"

Longarm frowned thoughtfully. "Yeah, that's who *I'd* pick if I was a snake in the garden trying to cause as much trouble as I could. Who gossips so mean, Doc? Male or female, I mean to have a serious word with the person."

Purvis said, "I forbid you to embarrass my wife. And, even if you do, she won't tell you. Nobody would report to her if she broke her word about keeping confidences."

"I get the picture. I was wondering why she wandered about so during trail stops. She naturally told you she has to talk private to others a lot, Doc?"

Purvis nodded. "Of course. I can't be everywhere, and there are things the other wives would only confide to another woman. Now that you know we know about you and the Hansen woman, what do you propose to do about it?"

Longarm said, "Nothing. I ain't been fooling with Inga Hansen, and my code forbids me to either screw or beat up a mean-hearted bitch."

"I hope that was not my wife you were referring to, sir. I know you're bigger and younger than me, but . . ."

"Oh, don't get your bowels in an uproar, Doc. If your wife says she was only passing the word on, I can't accuse her of making it up. You have my man-to-man word *somebody* made it up, though. For I've never even considered Inga as a conquest, pretty as she is. Her *hus-*

band is prettier than me, as well as too big to mess with."

Purvis started to say something about Gus Hansen. Then he looked away. "Well, you've been warned. If you intend to stay with this party, I'd better not hear any more about it."

Longarm was too polite to contradict his elders. He turned on his heel and marched over to the wagons. He found Von Thaldorf seated on a wagon tongue, talking with Bradford. He told the Austrian, "You, come with me. We got to talk."

As both started to rise, Longarm told Bradford, "Not you, him. It's private."

He led the Austrian out on the bare playa, turned, and said, "I just had a mighty odd conversation with Doc Purvis. His wife just told him I've been messing with the Hansen woman. How come?"

The other lawman tried to bluff the opening hand by asking how on earth *he* should know a thing about the private conversations of a married couple.

Longarm said, "Before you screw yourself so deep in the ground I have to call you a liar, I may as well 'fess up I know about you and Martha Purvis."

Von Thaldorf looked incredulous and replied, innocent-eyed, "Me and that elderly peasant women? How droll! The gossip about you and the Hansen woman makes more sense, don't you agree?"

Longarm shook his head. "No. I've never even smiled at Inga Hansen and I've seen you with Martha Purvis. She tells her husband she's off playing morals detective at such times. I figured she had to be telling him *something* to account for her vanishing acts."

Von Thaldorf looked sheepish. *"Zum Teufel,* a man

has needs, and she says Purvis is not the man in bed he once was, so . . ."

"I don't care about her," Longarm said. "It's the way she's been using her mouth that concerns me. I want you to tell her to straighten the matter out about me and Inga Hansen. Why'd you let her do it in the first place? What in thunder did either me or Gus Hansen ever do to you?"

The Austrian blanched and said, *"Herr Gott,* I told her *not* to repeat any such gossip to her husband. I have some experience in court intrigues. So I told her the first rule in conducting a discreet affair was never to mention sex to the old goat wearing the horns."

"I can see you're an old hand at the game, Von Thaldorf. Let's get back to who *told* your play partner I was hanging horns on Gus Hansen."

The Austrian shrugged. "It certainly wasn't me. Had I even guessed the Hansens were having trouble I would have never wasted my youth on an older and less attractive woman, *nicht wahr?"*

"All right. Who says the Hansen woman might be up for grabs?"

"Inga herself. She asked Martha whether, as the wife of a doctor, she knew any cure for impotence. It seems our Gus has a drinking problem, and his quiet but steady drinking causes problems for his young and healthy wife. Martha told Inga the only cure for Inga's condition was another man."

"I've heard the same thing, from gals who was once married to drunks. But where in hell do *I* fit in? I sure hope I wasn't suggested as a cure?"

The Austrian laughed and said, "As a matter of fact, I offered *my* discreet services, when Martha told me

121

about the problem. She said she'd scratch my eyes out if I even looked at poor Inga. She asked if I thought you might be the one to help Inga out. I told her I didn't think we ought to approach you on the matter. Forgive me, my young American friend, but you have never struck me as a very sophisticated type."

Longarm said, "I ain't, if pure dangerous adultery is what they call sophisticated at the court of Franz Josef. But never you mind my personal views. Just make sure the gossip about me and the Hansen woman comes to a total halt. If you had the brains of a gnat you'd cut out all that sophistication with the Purvis woman as well. The Doc had enough sand in his craw to stand up to me about *another* man's woman. Did he find out someone was messing with his *own,* I'd have to arrest the survivor, this being federal land, and I got enough to worry about."

Von Thaldorf frowned. "I hardly think that silly old man could beat me in a duel, Longarm."

"I hardly think so, neither," Longarm said. "That's why it would be cold-blooded murder, and there's limits to the professional courtesy I've been ordered to extend to you, Colonel."

Von Thaldorf stared soberly at Longarm. "Do you really think you could presume to arrest *me,* Herr *Deputy* Marshal?" he asked.

Longarm shrugged and said, "I'd have to try, even though I've seen how good you shoot. So don't gun the old man and, unless you're serious about gunning me, don't hover that hand so menacing near your holster, Colonel. I can't give men as good as you an edge. So don't look as if you mean to draw unless you really mean it."

The Austrian looked startled, raised his gun hand to stare down at it sort of surprised, and said, *"Zum Teufel, why are we arguing about mere women? Before you brought me out here to discuss such unimportant matters, I was going over that gunfight we had at the water hole the other day with Bradford."*

"How come? He ran off before he could have noticed much."

"I was too courteous to mention that to him. As you know, his older and braver brother spent some hours with us that day, in Bradford's wagon. They discussed those outlaws in depth. The brothers know the towns at both ends of the trail as only mail deliverers can. There has never been a letter addressed to a Turner, and was not that other outlaw you shot in Rosebud Wash named Taylor?"

Longarm nodded. "Spuds Taylor. You just noticed? I been over that in my head some, ever since that water hog introduced his fool self by a similar name."

He reached for a smoke as he explained, "It works too many ways to waste brain sweat on. The late Jake Turner could have been an unimaginative relative of the late Spuds Taylor. Spuds said he had kin waiting for him up the trail. After that it slopes the other way. Neither name is all that rare, and everybody gives *some* fool name or another. Turner and his gang was camped mighty far up the trail indeed to be waiting on an escaped cousin, and he was acting sort of brazen for a gent running a desert hideout."

He thumbed a match head aflame, lit his cheroot, and added, "It hardly matters one way or the other, now, since all concerned is dead as they could get if I delivered one and all to the hangman."

Von Thaldorf twisted an end of his waxed moustache thoughtfully. "We are not permitted to close the books on wanted criminals so casually," he said. "I had not considered how far that gang was from Rosebud Wash, frankly. Have you forgotten that someone tried to murder us by destroying that sign posted at the poison well?"

Longarm blew a smoke ring, admiring it in the bright desert sunlight. "They may not have been out to murder us all that personal," he replied. "The water hogs could have done it, hoping to improve business. An Indian or an illiterate white could have wanted some wood for kindling, meaning no harm at all. You sure worry a lot about loose ends for a peace officer, Colonel. I've found that once you bring a crook in with enough evidence to convict him, he generally gets around to the full story of his life by the time they spring the trap under him. Men in jail don't have much to do but talk."

He glanced up at the sun and said, "Men standing on an open desert under a rising sun has better things to do than bullshit. I'm fixing to haul some water and get under some shade."

Chapter 8

The next few camp and trail stops had Longarm so tensed for trouble both the young gals he was fooling with commented on it. He told neither Tess nor Doris why he had an ear cocked for gunfire, no matter what they were doing.

But save for the one day the Stoner boy ran off after rabbit with his .22, stepped in crusted-over alkali, and lost some toenails as well as his popgun, the last leg of the journey was just hot and tedious. Longarm couldn't tell whether Von Thaldorf had broken off with Martha Purvis or had just told her to be more careful. Longarm didn't catch her screwing or mean-mouthing him any more. He wouldn't have known if Inga Hansen was flirting with him or not, since he made sure he never went anywhere near the big blonde. He did notice, now that he had been alerted to the notion, that it was she, not her husband, who drove their wagon on the trail at night. He didn't ask her why.

Then one morning, as the sun was threatening to rise and Longarm was about to order another halt, he heard a distant bugle raising a distant flag and muttered, "Son of a bitch. We're there."

It still took an hour and a half to really get there, with the last half hour unbearable. But Longarm couldn't have held the others back if he'd wanted to. He rode ahead, once it seemed obvious there was no way even Bradford could get them lost within simmering sight of the red, white, and blue.

Fort Bidwell itself was a glorified observation post manned by a platoon under a first lieutenant turning gray in the service. Washington didn't spend much on the army, considering its Indian policy.

Indians, gamblers, whores, and such weren't allowed to squat smack on the post parade, of course, so a shantytown bigger than the post itself had grown up outside the adobe walls but sharing the awful water from what was called the upper alkali lake when it wasn't dried out totally.

As he rode for the garrison gate, Longarm saw an Indian women in a mother hubbard and lip rouge staggering barefoot down the dusty street, too drunk to feel how hot the sun was beating her over the head. Longarm grimaced and told his mule, "I wish we didn't do that to them. I wouldn't bring *my* band in, neither, if I was Ho."

The guard on duty at the gate waved them through

once Longarm flashed his badge. First things having to come first, he rode to the stables and signed a statement of charges for the army mule he had lost. Then he asked the remount sergeant if he could borrow two fresh ones, going back. They asked when he wanted them. He said he would hand-carry his gear and such from the wagons once he took care of more important business.

He went to the telegraph office and wired Billy Vail where he was. Then he took out the official dossier Von Thaldorf had lent him and told the army telegrapher, "I need someone as can read this for me, Corporal."

The telegrapher looked at the now somewhat battered sheaf of paper and said, "This looks to be writ in *German,* Deputy."

Longarm said, "I noticed. I'd be more worried if the Austro–Hungarian police kept their records in Algonquin. No offense, but half the recruits you get these days are German if they ain't Irish. Do you reckon you could find me a German-talking dragoon who can write it down in English for me as well?"

The young noncom said he could try. Longarm said he would be in the orderly room or officers' club, depending on how hospitable their First John was, if and when they could get the fool thing translated for him.

He went to the orderly room and caught the C.O. buttoning up his blues. He said, "You didn't have to get up for me, Lieutenant. With your permission, I can get all I need, here, from your enlisted help."

The officer wanted to know what he was talking about. So, as he poured a couple of tumblers of Maryland rye, Longarm brought him up to date. The officer poured more heat medication and sat on the corner of his desk, exhausted by the effort. He shook his head. "I

127

fear you've ridden all this way on a fool's errand, as far as that Krinke jasper goes. You say you ran into possible deserters from this post as well?"

Longarm got out the I.D. he had recovered from the rascals at the miner's cabin and handed them over. The lieutenant glanced at the names. "So much for that, then. I'll tell my first sergeant he can remove them from the post T.O. You know, of course, there's a standing bounty on deserters?"

Longarm nodded, but said, "I ain't allowed to claim reward money, and that Indian gal would only get in trouble with it. Let's get back to *other* runaways. I can see you're a man who pays attention to things on or about your post, so I'll take your word Hans Krinke never joined the army. But what about the riffraff camped all about, outside?"

The officer grimaced. "I have my men keeping an eye on them. We're only allowed to arrest 'em when they do something serious. Most of my men draw no more than thirteen dollars a month, so there aren't too many of the pests and, while some have moved *out* since spring, nobody has moved *in*, to my knowledge, this side of the Glorious Fourth."

Longarm thought and said, "That's too far back for Krinke. But I'd best ask about, anyways. Who's the bully of the camp who'd know everyone out there?"

"They call him Bully Brown, of course. He's a one-eyed thug, run out of Angel's Camp for cheating at cards. They say he rakes in the pot no matter how the cards are dealt. We had a serious discussion about his future here after he beat up a couple of my men. He says he's reformed. If you talk to him, watch out for the bowie he has strapped to the small of his back. He knows I don't have much authority about purely civilian arguments."

Longarm said he would and wistfully inquired whether the officers' club was off limits to civilians. The lieutenant sighed and said, "I'm the only officer on this post. I've never gotten around to organizing my own club. You're welcome to drink here as long as you like. I'll leave the bottle. I'd invite you to join me in my quarters, but my Modoc roommate is sort of shy."

Longarm thanked him and let him go. He moved around to the far side of the desk and sat down, pouring himself another drink. So the blond bullet-headed private who came in next looked down at him sort of startled and saluted.

Longarm said, "I don't rate a salute, and the man who does ain't here. Do you want a drink, old son?"

The private looked even more surprised. "If it please *mein herr,* I am Trooper Reisenfeld, and I have here a typed translation of some papers in German written."

Longarm said in that case he *had* to have a drink with him. "I been trying to go over that dossier for days," he explained. "I suspect the gent as gave it to me might have a sardonic sense of humor."

He got rid of the helpful German–American with half a tumbler of rye and settled back to read the dossier. He was just about finished when Von Thaldorf came in and said, "I have been looking all over for you. Krinke is not here. He never *has* been here. You were right. The fox has back on his own trail doubled!"

Longarm nodded at the bottle on the desk between them. "I figured he might have. I wish I'd read this sooner, Colonel. For now I see we was slickered deliberate by a false-hearted woman. I don't mean Martha

129

Purvis. I'm talking about a lady you have down here as Krinke's woman, under the name Hilda Horthy."

Von Thaldorf sat down, helping himself to the bottle and the empty tumbler left by the other officer. "What of it?" he said. "Of course he has lady friends in Vienna. So do I."

Longarm said, "Says here Fraulein Horthy is a natural redhead of Hungarian extract. Hungarians call themselves Magyar, right?"

"Of course. We've already been over that. What does it matter what our missing Hans's lover calls herself? I have no warrant for her arrest, even if she was in this country."

"She is," said Longarm flatly. "For I went swimming with her just outside Rosebud Wash, the more fool I, and she slipped up on that Magyar business, even though she said she was a plain old Vienna pastry, raised to call 'em *Ungers*."

"Herr Gott! That little communist was in Rosebud Wash while I was there?"

Longarm shook his head. "She come in by stage after me. By the way, would you know her on sight, like Krinke?"

Von Thaldorf shook his head and said, "No. As you see, she is only as a known associate of Krinke listed. I had no reason to suspect she might be here in America."

"Let me guess about the so-called police informant you met in Rye Patch, then," Longarm said. "I don't suppose it could have been a Hungarian lady, patriotic to old Franz Josef, even if her folk ain't noted for it?"

"That's ridiculous," the Austrian said. "The Hungarian waitress who came forward for the reward had jet-black hair, and . . . *Ach, Gott!*"

Longarm nodded. "Don't feel so bad. She slickered me with her hair left *natural*. That little red fox fed us both a red herring, Colonel. She sent you up the Siwash Trail after nobody much, and then she tried to convince me, as well, with a pathetic tale of political persecution. I owe the State Department an apology for even wondering if her tale could be true. Going over her boyfriend's record in more detail, I can see he's one bad apple. He prints fake passports for political radicals for *money,* not an undivided admiration for any particular cause."

Von Thaldorf brushed an imaginary fly away from the air between them. "That part is no mystery. That *redhead* is what concerns me now. How can you be sure you met Hilda Horthy if neither of us can be sure what she looks like in the flesh?"

Longarm said, "Nothing's sure but death and taxes, Colonel. But guesswork is allowed on this job. It's possible Krinke has two red-headed admirers who speak Hungarian as a first lingo when they ain't paying attention to German and English they learned later. But just how *probable* would you say it was?"

The Austrian heaved a great sigh. "Such a fool I feel," he said. "I gave her five hundred of your dollars for telling me she'd seen Krinke board the stage for Rosebud Wash."

Longarm nodded. "They likely had use for the money. The Frisco Palace is expensive, and it might take them some time to set up shop there. I didn't find meeting up with her so expensive. But if it's any comfort, I sure feel dumb, too. When things are too good to be true, they generally are."

The Austrian poured himself another drink, a stiff one, and asked what they could do next.

"To begin with, we have to get back down to the railroad," Longarm said.

"Herr Gott, all the way back to Rye Patch, along that same cursed trail?"

Longarm said, "Not before it gets dark again. By now you may have noticed the short way on the map ain't always the quickest way on the ground. So even though we're over the California line on the map, going back to the rails and riding most of the way by steam has any *other* way to Frisco beat."

"I can see that," sighed the Austrian, "but I swore I'd never ride that damned Siwash Trail again!"

Longarm nodded. "So did I. If it was one bit worse, nobody could make it at all, that way. It won't be so bad, going back by way of the *right* one."

Von Thaldorf blinked owlishly at him. "What right way?" he asked. "Are you suggesting there might be *another* trail? A *better* one?"

Longarm nodded. "Yeah, and I deserve a horsewhipping for being so stupid. But, to tell the truth, it never crossed my mind until I'd spent some time with Ho and listened to them jaw some."

"What on earth are you talking about? Did those Indians tell you about another trail?"

"Not directly. The old Digger as told the whites about it, or tried to, was from another band. How he wound up dead is too tedious to go into at this late date. But it's obvious why the one white man who talked any Indian at all called him a Siwash, or trash Indian. He was a mean drunk, disgusted by the trouble he had understanding an old man answering in another lingo entire. The mountain man was ashamed to allow he didn't know as much Indian as he let on. So he picked up on words that seemed to make a *little* sense, at least. The old man never called one trail the cattle and the other salty. He said *Ka-atle,* meaning No Water, and *Saltu,* meaning a trail suited to sissy white men. There ain't a trail possible with no water at *all,* so when they surveyed his *cattle trail* they just put it down as enthusiasm on the part of a dumb old Indian who'd never herded cows. They took his word the Saltu Trail was salty, and never tried it at all."

Von Thaldorf frowned thoughtfully and said, "That is a most interesting theory, Longarm. But, even if it's true, how does one find the *north* end of your mysterious Saltu Trail? To ride back all the way to where it branches off the one we just followed seems to be a pointless task, *nicht wahr?"*

"We don't have to find it," Longarm said. "Silas Bradford knows the way and, if he knows what's good for him, he'll show us. So far, all I got on him is sharp business practice."

The Austrian started to rise. Longarm said, "Sit down. It's hot as hell out, now. Silas ain't much, but he's too smart to ride out across the alkali flats this side of sundown. I figure the two trails rejoin somewhere near that water hole where we had the shootout with the water hogs. So it don't really matter whether he's willing to show us or not."

Von Thaldorf started to ask a dumb question. But he was a good hunter, too. So he nodded and said, "Of course, that is where his *brother* joined us! They have been using the shorter and better trail in secret to keep their mail contract monopoly, *nicht wahr?"*

Longarm nodded. "The younger one contracted to lead the Purvis party the long, dry way, lest someone else scout wider, and trip over their family secret. I noticed Silas didn't know the official route much better than anyone else. The lady running the stage station in Rosebud Wash said the Bradford boys had outbid her line on the mail contract, no doubt shortly after they gave the so-called Salty Trail a try for the hell of it, maybe in winter, and saw what the old wounded Ho really *meant*."

The Austrian asked how many miles Longarm thought the real cutoff saved. Just before Longarm could explain what a dumb question that was they both heard a long, low drum roll outside. Von Thaldorf asked, "Could that be thunder?"

"They'd hardly be holding a parade with the C.O in the sack and the mercury so far up," Longarm said. "It happens, now and again, out here. Clouds can't roll over the mountains to the west without considerable fuss. Hope it don't rain, though. Summer rain complicates a desert crossing considerable."

"Are you crazy? A good shower is just what we need to cool things off, Longarm."

Longarm poured another drink. "An *indoor* shower is just what I could use right now. Steam-bathing across flooded alkali gumbo can get tedious as hell."

The Austrian stared out the office window. "*Ach,* so dark it is all of a sudden getting!"

Longarm swore. "We're in for it, now, sure as hell."

But as it suddenly began to rain fire and salt he followed the needlessly overjoyed Austrian out on the veranda, leaving the office and almost half the bottle to its original owner.

The parade out front was already flooded inches deep. Whooping dragoons were prancing around on it in their underwear or less as the rain streamed over their long-overheated hides. Longarm told his fellow lawman, "Don't do that. It could all be over before noon and you'd bake like a clam in wet duds."

Von Thaldorf nodded. "I am already feeling cooler. The air is in fact getting *cold*. Such a crazy climate you have in your Wild West!"

Longarm lit another smoke under the overhang. "It ain't quite this crazy all over," he said. "But this does change our plans some. If it rains more than a few minutes—and it looks like it's planning to—we won't be riding after dark like I said. So it ain't as important to sleep this afternoon. Hot or cold, we dasn't risk open desert changed total by less'n half a moon. So we may as well turn in tired, after giving the taxpayers an honest day's work for a change. I got more wires to send, now that my brain's starting to work. You want to wire your embassy while we're at a post where the sending is free?"

Von Thaldorf said it hardly mattered, since he always sent wires collect and hadn't caught Krinke yet. Longarm left him to watch the kids at play and followed the overhang down to the army telegraph post.

As he was composing a fuller report in his head Longarm asked the clerk on duty whether the wires ran due east across the nothing-much or whether they were patched into the main cross-country lines by way of Sacramento. The clerk said the latter worked as well and asked why it mattered. Longarm said, "Just covering all bets. I didn't expect nobody to cut your line on

135

the desert between here and where I'm headed next, but it's always nice to know they can't."

He wrote a longer than usual report to Denver, considered sending it day rates, anyhow, since some of the information was important, and decided night letter rates would do, considering how long it took to cross deserts, even the shorter ways.

When he rejoined Von Thaldorf the rain seemed to be letting up, but the sky was staying overcast as a whopping wet-wool blanket. When the Austrian opined it looked like they were in for an all-day storm, Longarm nodded morosely. "Yeah, I sure hope it ain't coming down like this over beyond the Black Rock Range. No matter how the Saltu cutoff runs, she's got to cross that big fat playa between us and Rosebud Wash."

Von Thaldorf said, *"Ach,* even so, it shall many days take us to get back that far, even by a shorter route. How long can it take the Black Rock Desert to bake dry again?"

"The *crust?* No time at all, once the sun's out again. After that, crossing a playa gets as safe as skating on thin ice for *weeks,* after a real summer rain."

He looked up at the sky, saw no change, and decided, "Long as it ain't coming down right now, I figure I'll drift over to the shantytown and double-check on old Krinke. You want to tag along, or do you want to meet me at the wagons later?"

"To the wagons we have to go, if only to get our things," the Austrian said. "Do you really think Krinke could be among such riffraff hiding?"

"Not unless I owes a certain redhead an apology. But I like to cover all bets, when I got the time, and I hate long goodbyes. Purvis already said he aimed to rest up here a few days before pushing on for the Applegate. I ain't up to a whole afternoon as well as a whole night of resting up in the Grover wagon. So I'll meet you later."

Von Thaldorf headed over to the stable to get his own riding mount. Longarm didn't. The shantytown was just outside the gate, the wagon train was camped less than a quarter of a mile out, and a man fought better in strange surroundings on his feet. So Longarm walked.

The inhabitants of the canvas-and-tarpaper rabbit warren were only human, so they were outside marveling at the break in the heat, too. Some had forgotten to get dressed properly for the occasion. Longarm asked a whore with rain-streaked face paint where he could find Bully Brown. She flashed gold teeth at him and said, "You don't want to see Bully Brown, handsome. You look too young and pretty to die. What say you come inside with me and let me show you something nicer?"

He smiled down at her politely. "I thank you kindly for such consideration, ma'am, but I got to talk to the bully of this camp."

She shrugged her naked shoulders. "Swing left at that tarpaper job down the line and look for a circus-tent saloon called the Desert Rose. Don't say who sent you if Bully asks. I don't know why I'm being so nice to you, big spender."

Longarm was too polite to suggest he might remind her of a long-lost son. As he swung the corner he heard her whistle sharply with her fingers between her gold teeth. He wasn't surprised when a gent as tall as him and twice as broad across hove into view well this side of the big canvas tent to demand his name and business with Bully Brown in the flesh.

Longarm smiled politely but said, "It won't work.

137

They told me the one and original Bully Brown wears a patch over one eye, and you don't. But I ain't such a big fibber. So I'll tell you I'm a deputy U. S. marshal and then you'll tell me where the man I'm looking for might be, won't you?"

The moose turned his head to call out, "Hey, Bully? We got us a real wise-ass, here. Says he's law and just calt me a liar!"

Another, even bigger cuss came out of the big tent, followed by a cur-dog pack of seven men and four painted gals. The genuine one-eyed article packed two guns, slung low, and Longarm had been warned about the bowie he was more reluctant to display. Bully Brown shoved his chest out and moved closer than was polite to see if Longarm would take the usual instinctive step backward. He didn't. He said, "I hope you ain't aiming to kiss me, Brown, for I ain't that sort of a gent."

One of the whores giggled as Brown took the step back for breathing room and growled, "All right. Spike says you're law. I ain't done a thing deserving of a federal warrant, and there *ain't* no township law here. I ain't got around to running for sheriff yet."

Longarm said, "I know. Army told me how smart you've been. I ain't here to pester you and yourn, Bully. I'm hunting a foreigner called Hans Krinke. He'd hardly be using that name these days. He's shorter than you, which only stands to reason, but taller than most gents. He's got brown hair and ordinary features. He's Austrian, so he talks funnier than you or me. Am I wasting your time, or could he have been through here in the recent past?"

Brown shook his head and said, "Lucky for you, he

ain't. I don't think much of furriners, so I'd recall beating up such a critter if he'd been here. I can see you're a real American as well as braver than most. So what can we do for you? We got women, likker, and various games of chance on tap for your pleasure."

"If you don't like girls, Bully will be proud to bend over for you," one of the whores added.

Brown didn't kill her, so Longarm knew the bully had a sense of humor, or the whore was grand in bed. Nobody else laughed, so Longarm didn't. "I ain't got the change to spare, thanks. I didn't think our want could be here, but I had to check. Now that I has, I'll be on my way."

Brown asked, "Where are you staying? We can make you a lot more comfortsome than that army post, even if you only needs an empty bed. We shoot bedbugs on sight and nobody's allowed to steal in this camp without my permission."

Longarm explained, "I got a place to bed down tonight, thanks. I come in with that wagon train and they're fixing to stay over a few days while they rest their critters and wait for another guide to take 'em west on the army trace."

Brown nodded. "In that case I'd best pay 'em a visit later. If they're camped on township ground and drinking township water, they owes us *money*."

Longarm shook his head. "Leave 'em alone, Bully. They been through enough of late. I don't want 'em rawhided."

"Now who said anything about rawhiding anybody, Uncle Sam? You surely can't expect me to let 'em squat for free?"

Longarm's smile grew thinner as he replied, "I

wasn't going to bring this up, but since you did, you drifters are the ones who are squatting, free, on federal land. There ain't no incorporated township here, Brown. A tolerant U. S. Army has let you camp here on land it has no other use for. You got no more legal status than a band of reasonably friendly Indians. That wagon party has the same rights. No more. No less. So don't mess with 'em. I mean it."

Brown started to argue. Longarm didn't see any sense in listening. He turned and walked away. Behind him, he heard a whore ask the bully if he meant to let anyone talk to him like that. He heard her getting slapped good, too. So it was likely over.

Chapter 9

The wagon camp was more active by daylight than it had been in recent memory. Half the adults were still taking advantage of the break in the heat to catch up on their sleep, but some were up and about, and all the kids were playing leapfrog or mud pies, depending on age. Some enlisted men from the post had drifted over to see if they could be of service. Two of them were flirting with the Grover girls at the moment. Longarm looked the other way and headed for the Purvis wagon to explain things to the Doc. Von Thaldorf's mount was tethered to a hind wheel. That didn't surprise Longarm as much as the noises he heard through the canvas as he got closer. He swore and softly called, "Get out here on

141

the double, Colonel! Have you gone frothing-at-the-mouth insane?"

Von Thaldorf climbed out, not bothering with his hat and coat, to inform Longarm the expedition leader was over at the army post, buying fresh provisions and trying to make a deal with a new guide. Longarm said, "I didn't think he was in there with you and his wife. You sure must enjoy living dangerously. What's the story on Bradford? I don't see his wagons here, now."

The Austrian said, "They were not here when I got back. One of the children said he left during the rainstorm. I assume he must be in a hurry to get back to Rye Patch, *nicht wahr?*"

Longarm said, "He's still got more sense than *you,* if he bogs in alkali. Get anything as ain't already lashed to your mule and consider leaving as soon as the Doc gets back. I have to warn him about possible trouble with a local tough as I say my proper goodbye."

"But you said it might be dangerous to cross the alkali flats in the dark now, Longarm."

"I know what I said. We'll make camp out on a drier part of the trail once it's dark. I can see it's time to get you out of here before you press your luck past dumb to crazy. I ain't as sure as I once was whether *I* was meant to spend the night here, neither. I'd best haul my pack saddle over to the army stable before things get awkward. Meet me there within the hour. Don't tell Martha you might not be coming back. You're sure to get caught if she insists on saying goodbye her way."

Von Thaldorf laughed and climbed back up into the Purvis wagon. Longarm swore and headed across camp. He swore again, louder, when he saw his pack saddle neatly draped over the wagon pole in front of the closed canopy. Neither the Grover sisters nor the two soldiers they'd been jawing with were in sight. He tried to get really sore, gave it up with a sheepish chuckle, and muttered, "Just as well. I only gave myself an hour."

He stopped to light a fresh cheroot. A timid hand plucked his sleeve and he turned to see Inga Hansen standing there in her bare feet and thin calico mother hubbard. The dress was shapeless, but it didn't hide much when a gal was built like the curvaceous blonde. He ticked the brim of his Stetson to her and asked if he could be of service to her, quickly adding, "Don't see your man around, Miss Inga."

She said, "He's in the wagon, dead drunk. Is it true you are riding back to the railroad, Custis?"

He said it was.

"Take me with you," she said. "All I have to offer is my body, but I can't go on with Gus. I have to go home to my own people, even if I have to sell myself to get there."

Longarm gulped and told her, "You ain't talking sensible, no offense. Once you get to Oregon, things may look better. Even if they don't, you can still write home for money and get back more decent."

"I can't stand him," she said. "He never bathes, even when there's water. He beats me, too."

Longarm said, "Hit him back. You're a big gal and you ought to be able to hold your own, sober. Your notion of riding back with the colonel and me is dumb, Miss Inga."

"Don't you *want* me? You must have heard the gossip. It's already cost me some bruises. I'd as soon have the game as just the name."

Longarm sighed and said, "Lord have mercy and

give me strength, for we both know what a glorious game it would be. You're a mighty handsome woman, and I'm only human. But *somebody* has to use some common sense. I can't take you with us. I want to. It just won't work."

"You'd leave me here, undefended, in the hands of a brute?"

"Oh, he can't be *that* brutal, or he'd have bruised me instead of you, girl. Wife beaters is usually weaker than they let on, even when they hit women sober. Just hit him back now and again. Or, hell, take an axe to him. But get to Oregon somehow before you make serious plans on abandoning all you've worked for to go whoring off across the desert."

She told him she was mighty disappointed in his manhood and turned away, crying. As he watched her go his manhood said it was never going to forgive him.

The Austrian had said Doc Purvis was over at the post. There was little sense waiting on him here. He moved over to the Grover wagon to pick up his pack saddle. He waved back at some muddy kids who waved at him and headed out. That would have been the end of his association with the Purvis party had he not seen Bully Brown and his rat pack moving in. Longarm dropped the pack saddle and got between it and the advancing thugs as he called out, "The man in command ain't here and, even if he was, I told you not to pester these folk, Brown."

The bully looked innocent. "Now who said we was here to pester pilgrims, Uncle Sam?" he asked.

"Me. They got water. Their stock is grained. The sutler at the post sells trail gear and supplies at a tolerable price if he aims to keep his government license, so there's nothing you can sell 'em, and you're still facing the wrong way, Brown."

"It's a free country. I guess a man has the right to go anywhere he wants to, Uncle Sam."

Longarm shook his head. "Not when I tell him not to. I don't mean to argue law with you, Brown. The only law you understand is barnyard, and I already told you this ain't your dung heap. So turn around and get back on your own dung heap, now, or fill your fist."

Bully Brown looked hurt. "Is that any way to talk when you're outnumbered seven to one, Uncle Sam?" he asked.

A voice behind Longarm said, "You are wrong. It is seven against *two*, you unwashed one-eyed creature."

Longarm said, "Stay out of this, Von Thaldorf. I can handle it."

Bully Brown laughed and said, "Oh, Lord have mercy, the prissy dude with the waxed moustache has a *Von* tacked on his prissy name! How do *we* git to be Vons, your Vonship?"

"To begin with, one must come from a good family," the Austrian said. "Why do you not go home and ask your mother who your father might have been? It's *possible* he was a passing gentleman, even though we know what *she* was, *nicht wahr?*"

Longarm groaned. "Hold on, damn it!" he said. Bully Brown slapped leather. Neither he nor Longarm had their guns out as Von Thaldorf's dragoon roared and the bully doubled over and went down, gasping, "Jesus Christ! I've been kilt!"

Longarm covered the others, none of whom did anything surly with their gun hands. "That's the whole show, boys," he snapped. "You got ten seconds to get out of sight, and it's open as hell around here."

They took the hint and started running. Longarm waited until they were out of pistol range before he turned to Von Thaldorf and said, "Don't do that no more. How do you feel right now, Brown?"

The bully sat in the mud, both hands gripping his paunch as blood leaked through his fingers, and groaned, "I am shot in the heart and I'll never forgive you. What's the matter with you gents? Can't you take a little joshing?"

Longarm said, "Never slap leather on a man who calls your mother mean things unless you mean it, Brown. Just sit tight. That gunshot must have carried to the army post, and I know for a fact there's at least one doctor there."

In no time at all they were surrounded by men in blue as well as some kids from the wagon train. Longarm shooed the kids back. A burly sergeant asked what was up and Longarm said, "He ain't up. He's down, with a no-doubt long-overdue pistol ball in him. I want you to carry him to the post dispensary and make sure he lives. For I ain't got time to fill out all the papers if he don't."

The sergeant asked who the hell he thought he was. Longarm flashed his badge. "Don't mess with me, Sergeant. It's starting to warm up again, and I ain't got time for dumb arguments."

The sergeant told a couple of privates to help the wounded man to his feet. "I figured someone had to, shoot this one sooner or later. Come on, Bully Brown, you ain't hurt that bad, and you're too big to carry."

Brown protested, "I needs a stretcher, damn it. Can't

you see I'm wounded bad? No shit, boys, it hurts like hell when I breathe."

They told him not to breathe, then, as they started to stagger him away. Longarm turned back to the Austrian who had gunned him. "We'd have been stuck here for days if you'd killed him for sure. As it is, he still might die. So let's get the hell *out* of here!"

Chapter 10

It wasn't easy. The C.O. wanted them to hang around until he knew whether to report the matter as a shanty-town brawl or justifiable homicide. Longarm finally convinced him a man that big ought to live with less than a pound of lead in him, and that even if he died, nobody was ever likely to make a fuss about it.

The two lawmen made eight or ten miles before sun-down under a dark sky and camped beside the trail they'd come in by. Longarm told the Austrian a fire was out of the question, not because of the climate but be-cause they were still close enough to Fort Bidwell for Bully Brown's friends to hunt them, if they really meant to.

Von Thaldorf said he was just being fussy, but turned in without arguing, once they'd polished off plenty of beans and trade liquor mixed with canteen water.

Von Thaldorf used more water than Longarm thought wise the next morning, on the wrong side of his hide. Longarm awoke to catch him shaving and fussing with his appearance, even rewaxing his moustache. Longarm told him to treat water more sensibly in such surroundings. "The late James Butler Hickock was prissy about *his* appearance, along with other awful habits. I've never understood how gents who are so casual about messing other folk up can act so peacock about their *own* hides."

Von Thaldorf went on admiring himself in the little mirror from his fancy shaving kit and asked, "Are you accusing me of being a wanton killer? That sounds grotesque, coming from you, of all people."

Longarm sat up, rubbing his sleep-gummed face and stubble with a dry kerchief. "Bully Brown may live, if infection don't set in. I ain't saying you're wanton, pard. I'm just saying you shoot more casually than a good peace officer ought to. Next time you back my play, don't back it so noisy unless you see *me* slapping leather. Four times out of five I can talk my way through such discussions."

"Do you really concern yourself about the continued health of such scum?"

Longarm shrugged. "Scum got rights. More important, they sometimes *say* something if you give 'em a chance. I'm still in the dark about them water hogs we shot it out with, sooner than I was planning. They never got the chance to discuss their recent pasts with me. So I still ain't sure just how they fit into our future."

150

The Austrian put his kit back in a saddlebag, saying, "Since they are dead, I fail to see how the details of their criminal pasts can concern us now."

Longarm glanced up at the thinning overcast. "I didn't *think* a man who shaves with canteen water looks ahead too far. If we knew for a fact we could take the water hogs at face value, we could forget 'em, like you said. But nobody around Fort Bidwell could give me a line on 'em and you may have noticed they'd got to where we met up with them on *ponies*, not desert-hardy mules."

"*Ach*, surely horses can survive on this desert, within reason. What about your Wild West mustangs and Indian ponies?"

"I don't own either. There's horses running wild or even under Horse Utes, hither and yon in the Great Basin. But not as far from grass and water as mules. Them water hogs never reached that spring along the Siwash Trail, from either end."

"*Ach*, that is no mystery. You say yourself there must be another trail, a better one. The Bradford brother who came to our assistance must have been on it, perhaps the other side of the nearest ridge, when he—"

"When he *what?*" Longarm cut in, reaching for his boots. "He *said* he just happened along at a mighty convenient time. Try it this way. What if he was *with* them rascals?"

Von Thaldorf looked incredulous and said, "*Herr Gott*, he shot more of them than you and I put together, Longarm!"

"As well he should have, seeing as he had the drop on 'em, from behind. What if he was camped with 'em, saw his baby brother's red shirt about to get filled with

151

holes, and did what most big brothers might at such a time? He never backshot anybody *before* you pushed a heated business discussion into a shootout. I still ain't sure we'd have had one, had we handled it my way."

Von Thaldorf scowled. *"Ach,* next time I let you do it your way and send flowers. What on earth would that mail rider be doing in an outlaw camp?"

"Camping, of course. He was on his way down from Fort Bidwell on the secret Saltu cutoff, carrying mail, not money. Let's say he run into a gang of worse crooks, riding the other way along the same trail. If they'd been camped closer to Rosebud Wash, waiting for an escaped convict to join 'em, and given up after old Spuds failed to show in a reasonable time, they'd have headed north to such civilization as they could find, not back to Rosebud Wash, where whatever had happened to old Spuds must have happened. They took the Saltu Trail more or less by accident, not because they was so smart. Not knowing the country well, they'd never been told an old Indian had said the trail was salty. So they followed it, making good time, till they met Bradford. He wanted 'em to follow a better trail all the way to Fort Bidwell about as much as he wanted a dose of clap. So he slickered 'em by telling 'em, truthful enough, about that fine spring on an otherwise not-so-good trail. It was the late Jake Turner-or-Taylor's own notion to hog it, once he saw how good it was."

He rose, stretched, and said, "We can coffee and grub later, when we have to stop. Let's make a few miles before the sun busts through them clouds up yonder."

Von Thaldorf didn't argue, but as they were saddling

152

up he asked Longarm if there was any point to all this idle speculation about long-dead outlaws. "Yeah," Longarm said, "everything I just said was guesswork. Thanks to your boyish enthusiasm, I don't *know* a thing for sure. If I was sure the better trail led further north than that spring, we wouldn't have to ride all the way back to it to scout for it. We could beeline cross-country, direct."

As they mounted, Von Thaldorf gazed east across the featureless flats. "Why can't we just ride that way, then?" he asked.

Longarm shook his head. "Not hardly. It's easy enough to get lost on the desert *without* taking chances. There could be green pastures and still waters beyond that far horizon or there could be more nothing-much than here on a trail we know, shitty as it is. We'd best stay on her till we know for sure the other trail has to be close."

They rode down the Siwash Trail, taking advantage of the break in the heat to eat up some miles with a trot the mules could maintain without much trouble. Around noon, Longarm called a longer trail break to put away some beans and tomatoes, cold. The Austrian said it was the most disgusting lunch he'd enjoyed in some time, but he was a tolerable sport about it.

It was pushing three in the afternoon, and the sun had broken through to argue about it with them, when Longarm spied a pair of dots off the trail to the east, shimmering fuzzy in the desert air as the barren flats began to heat up again.

"I don't recall them wagons being there when we passed this way the other night," he told the Austrian.

"Be careful. Follow me at a walk, and if you see me bust through, back off."

As they rode out across the dried-over alkali crust, already crackle-glazed by the sun, they saw the wagon ruts ahead getting ever deeper. Longarm reined in when they were close enough to be sure. "Yep, I thought they looked like Bradford's lighter wagons. Don't see him or his stock bogged down. Don't see tracks coming back. He tried too soon after that rain."

The Austrian smiled grimly and said, "But he did go *on,* mounted. If we follow his spoor, it should take us to the better trail, *nicht wahr?*"

Longarm pointed southeast. "Don't have to follow him, bloodhound. Look at that smoke rising yonder."

A blue haze was blurring a considerable extent of the already fuzzy horizon. "That does not look like campfire smoke, Longarm. If I did not know it was impossible, I would say it had to be a *forest fire!*" Von Thaldorf exclaimed.

Longarm nodded and said, "It is, the son of a bitch. Let's go. Ground looks dried out more, that way, in any case."

As they rode gingerly across the treacherous alkali flat, Longarm explained how discouraging burnt-over grass and timber looked to a stranger at first glance. "The Diggers do it all the time to discourage Horse Utes from enjoying the comforts of their home," he said. "Bradford knows that after such a rain the slopes will green-up again in no time. Meanwhile, he's leaving scorched earth along the Saltu cutoff for the curious."

They rode toward the smoke. It was getting hotter by the minute, but Longarm said the sun would be down again before it could get as hot as usual out here. There was no shade to hole up in, anyway.

As the horizon ahead got more jagged, the Austrian glanced back the way they had come and gasped, "The flats behind us are flooding! How could that be? Where could all that water have sprung from?"

Longarm shot a casual glance at the shimmering expanse of mirage water to the west. "That's a break. If old Silas is scouting atop one of them hills ahead he won't see much. You always see such impossible sights with the sun ball facing you, pard. If you ever see a lake out here with the sun *behind* you, it's real. Rainbows work the opposing way. I don't see no rainbows over that range to our east, though, so we're likely in for more dry weather."

It took them the rest of the afternoon to reach an ever-rising range of sepia rock and smoking ash. Longarm shook his head. "Look what that piss-ant did to all that grass! And it takes years for piñon to grow back. The Ho will surely be pissed at old Silas if they ever discover who turned them pines along the ridge to burnt stumpwood."

Von Thaldorf nodded grimly. "You were right. He's turned this hillside to desert as ugly as it can appear!"

"Appearances is deceiving," Longarm said. "The ground water that carried the grass and scrub this far into summer is still there. *We* don't *need* water yet. We'd best grub and rest up here on the bare dirt for now. Ash is tedious to stumble about in, and the moon won't rise for hours tonight."

"Don't you want to press on after that villain, Longarm?"

155

"Why? We know where he's going, and the moon comes up twenty minutes later every night, remember?"

"Herr Gott, please don't explain the lunar calendar to me! Bradford can't be more than a few hours ahead of us, *nicht wahr?"*

Longarm dismounted. "Oh, he'll reach Rosebud Wash further ahead of us than that," he said. "He's riding with a guilty conscience and we'll be riding slow because it's a strange trail to us. His conscience may compel him to consider an ambush anywhere between here and there. I doubt he has the sand in his craw, but it pays to be careful, so I mean to. Don't worry, pard. Now that we've found the right way to get there, we'll likely get there sooner than either of us planned, taking it easy and enjoying the scenery."

Before midnight they found a water hole shimmering in the light of the now-quartering moon and enjoyed a dip before turning in beside it, despite the annoying fine ash. Longarm swam underwater and rinsed out his hair as well. He noticed his fellow traveler dog-paddled about with his backbone stiff as ever and his head held high, no doubt concerned about his moustache wax.

In the morning, Longarm scouted to the crest of the ridge and found a narrow, beaten track. Fresh mule droppings told him the way their firebug unwilling guide had preceded them.

It was cool enough along the ridge to ride by day. They kept their eyes peeled for a flash of red among the rocks ahead. They soon rode out of the burn. It was even nicer, riding among piñon, juniper, and short-grass greening near the root in the wake of the recent wet spell. From time to time the beaten path, no doubt laid out in the long-ago by Indians, dipped down off the ridges, mostly to the cooler eastern slopes, and every time it did they found water farther down, along with signs of unkempt camping. There were places where sweetwater actually sprang form the rocks to send little willow-haunted brooks down to die on the flats below.

Of course, to make up for this, there were stretches where the trail swung low, into hotter climes. But the misnamed Salty Trail always led them back to yet another well-watered ridge. Once, they crossed a fairly high one, dry as cobwebs, even along the top, and naturally Von Thaldorf had to ask why. Longarm explained, "Sandstone don't hold water. The wise old Ho run this trail across as much volcanic rock as possible. That's why it twists a mite. But we'll get there. We're saving miles as well as heatstroke, taking that poor old Indian's advice. It's no wonder he called this a Saltu, or white man's, trail. No wonder the Bradford brothers wanted to keep it a family secret, as well. I got a good mind to arrest them sons of bitches, once we catch up with 'em."

"*Herr Gott*, were you planning on doing anything *else*, once we meet those scoundrels?"

Longarm shrugged. "I reckon I could pin arsoning federal rangeland on old Silas, if I wanted to spend the time. But it would be hard to make her stick, and we still have to catch up with Hans Krinke so I can go on back to Denver. I'll tell Bull Culhane about it. He can do as he likes."

The Austrian frowned and objected, "Such a small-town police official would not have jurisdiction this far from his small town, would he?"

"Not hardly. Jurisdiction is tricky, even when you

think you got it. But once the others know what the Bradford boys has been hiding from them, that ought to be punishment enough. At the very least, if they ain't run out of town, they ought to lose their mail franchise. The stage line is better organized and ought to want it, once we tell 'em how easy it is to get from Rye Patch to Fort Bidwell after all."

It wasn't, in truth, as simple as all that. For, though they never spent more than a day away from water, and found grass even easier to find for their mules, they still had some bad stretches like the Black Rock Desert itself before, just as Von Thaldorf was getting broody about how long it was taking, they swung around a bend to find themselves near the big skull-shaped rock where the two trails divided outside of Rosebud Wash.

They agreed they were too close to stop now, so they rode on and made the little trail town around nine in the evening. Everyone in the Silver Spur seemed surprised to see them. Bull Culhane bought them beers and said, "Silas Bradford said you boys figured to show up a couple of weeks from now, if then."

Longarm swallowed a considerable gulp of beer before he put the schooner down on the bar. "I figured he expected us to come back the same way he so kindly led us up to Fort Bidwell. The colonel, here, can explain how we got back so sudden. The livery's taking care of what's left of our stock. I got to send some wires. I'll be back directly."

He went down to the Western Union. He sent a wire to his boss, Marshal Billy Vail, and picked up the reply to the messages he'd sent from Fort Bidwell. Billy said they had an all-points out on Hans Krinke and a certain redhead, confirming that the Austro–Hungarian Empire agreed that Herta Osterhoff and Hilda Horthy added up to one and the same person.

On the way back to the saloon, Longarm passed the stage station, glanced in, and saw the skinny little blond gal working on some papers at her counter. She looked prettier, by lamplight, this evening. He figured those nights on the trail with a scar-faced cuss had his glands going good by now. He passed on by. By morning the news would be all over town and she could do what she aimed to about the better mail route. He didn't have to tell her, and if he didn't keep an eye on that fool Austrian, he was likely to shoot somebody again.

When he reached the Silver Spur, Longarm saw he was already too late. The bar was cleared, with Von Thaldorf standing at one end, smiling thinly, and the two Bradford brothers at the other, closer to the back, not smiling at all.

Bull Culhane was just inside the batwings, out of the line of fire. The older Caleb Bradford asked the Austrian, "Are you calling me a liar, you sissy furriner?"

"Your town, Bull. How far do we let this go?" Longarm murmured.

"As far as it wants to," Culhane said. "If what that German gent just told us is true, they deserves gutshooting. If he just calt two local boys liars, and they ain't, *he* deserves a gutshooting."

Longarm sighed. "I'd best move up to stand beside the colonel, then, for I got to back his play as well as his words."

As he stepped into the light Von Thaldorf snapped, "Stay out of this, Longarm. It's my fight and, after all these unwashed louts just put me through, my *pleasure!*"

Longarm suggested mildly, "It's two on one, Colonel."

The Austrian laughed, not politely at all, and said, "I do not wish to make a habit out of calling everyone I meet a liar. But I do not think either of them has the courage."

Longarm stared judiciously. Silas looked as if he was about to piss his pants. Longarm told the older one, "You'd best back off, Caleb. The colonel won't, and he's sort of a ferocious gent."

"You stay out of this," said Caleb Bradford. "It's a private duel. My brother ain't in it neither. This is betwixt me and an asshole who uses moustache wax and calls growed men liars!"

The younger one almost whimpered as he chimed in, "You heard us, Longarm. You just stay out of my big brother's business if you know what's good for you."

Longarm muttered, "Shit," then told the Austrian, "Get it over with one way or the other before the whole town crowds in here, damn it. Buy the boys a drink or draw, for Pete's sake."

Von Thaldorf nodded and said, "*Ja,* one can see someone must, if this comedy is not to go on forever."

Without changing expression, he had a smoking gun in his fist and Caleb Bradford was on the floor, gripping his gut with both hands and screaming.

"You kilt my brother!" wailed Silas, tugging at the gun he wore inside his shirt. Von Thaldorf covered him, bemused. Then the gun jammed in the fool's shirt went off inside it, and Silas gasped, "Oh, Lord have mercy, I've kilt myself!"

They sent for the local vet after carrying the two blubbering Bradfords into the back room and stretching

160

them side by side on a pool table. The vet knocked them both out with opium and prepared to dig out the bullets.

Bull Culhane clapped Von Thaldorf on the back and said, "That was rare shooting, Colonel. It only cost you one bullet."

Everybody except Longarm seemed to think that was mighty amusing. Culhane said, "It serves 'em right. Is it true they slickered us all this time about the true trail north, Longarm?"

Longarm nodded, but told the Austrian, "It's a good thing you'll be heading back to Vienna town before either of 'em can be up and about again. I'd as soon kill a man, and take a chance with his kin, as leave him alive and no doubt mad as hell at me."

Von Thaldorf stared at the two forms on the pool table and put a casual hand on his gun grips. Longarm said, "Not *now*, damn it. I told you there was limits to how much professional courtesy I'm required to extend you."

Culhane nodded. "Leave 'em be, Colonel. You've punished 'em both as much as any man deserves to be punished." He turned to Longarm. "How long will you boys be in town, by the way?"

"We got to stay overnight. Maybe tomorrow, if it's really hot. *We* could likely take the ride to the railroad from here, but our critters couldn't," Longarm told him.

Culhane nodded and said he saw no need to worry about the matter, then. But Von Thaldorf worried Longarm by saying, "I am not by mule returning to Rye Patch. I hired my mount here. I shall leave him here and ride back in comfort, aboard the stage."

Longarm said, "I can't. I got to get the mules I borrowed off the army back to Fort Douglas. But I don't need the packings, now. What say you ride the spare mule, pard?"

Von Thaldorf grimaced. "Thank you, but I have ridden all the mules I care to, Longarm. I shall wait for you in Rye Patch, once the stage delivers me."

Longarm started to insist. Then he remembered Billy Vail had told him the fool foreigner was a guest of the federal government and not to rawhide him. Longarm sighed. "Well, I can't see myself dragging you kicking and screaming back across the salt flats, even if you *didn't* shoot so cruel. There ain't no stage tonight. I'm sort of tired. So we'll talk about it in the morning."

Culhane tried not to leer as he asked if Longarm meant to stay with the Widow Westbury again. Longarm shrugged. "I may have to, if I don't get cracking."

Chapter 11

He didn't go direct to ask old Babs if her shower still worked. He went back to the stage line's office and saw he had arrived just in time. The skinny blonde had just closed her ledger and put the stopper back on her ink-well when he stepped in. She looked up with a weary frown and said, "I was just about to close. The night stage left hours ago."

"I know. We can still do business. I want a ticket to Rye Patch, and how much would it cost me to have you folk lead two mules there in your own good time and leave 'em in the charge of Western Pacific for me?"

She said she'd have to study such an unusual deal.

"Was that you I heard shooting up the town a few minutes ago?" she asked.

He smiled. "Not this time. That's why I need a coach ticket. Every time I take my eyes off a foreigner I'm traveling with, he shoots somebody. Another gal who told some fibs about other matters told me the gent was a born killer. She wasn't lying about *that,* at least."

"Good heavens! Have we had another killing in Rosebud Wash?"

"Not exactly, but neither of the Bradford brothers will be carrying the mail for some time. So, if you still want to bid on that contract, you'd best do so, before anyone *else* does."

She started to tell him not to be silly. Her outfit had surveyed the Siwash Trail and given up on it.

"We just come down from Fort Bidwell fifty miles and a lot more water sooner, ma'am," he told her. "That Saltu cutoff everyone thought was salty is not only practical for coaching, it's better than the run from here to the railroad."

She looked startled but not at all displeased as she opened the gate in her counter and asked him to come back to her quarters and tell her all about it as she put some coffee and cake in him.

He didn't argue. She was skinny, but she sure smelled nice. She led him through a doorway, down a hall past another indoor bath, and just as he was expecting to have his coffee and cake in her kitchen, they wound up in a cozy room with a four-poster in one corner and a sofa facing a dead fireplace to make it seem less openly inviting. He tossed his hat aside and sat on the sofa, wishing he'd been neater about shaving on the trail.

164

She told him to go ahead and smoke as she ducked next door to fetch refreshments from her kitchen.

The cake was a mite stale and the coffee was neither warm nor iced, but she'd brewed real Arbuckle and said he could take all the sugar he wanted. He sipped it black as he brought her up to date since last they'd met, leaving out some parts about the redhead's swimming skills. The blonde said he could call her Irene and that the ride to Rye Patch would be on the house if half what he said about the new route was true. He asked her how much it was going to cost to get the mules back to Fort Douglas, and she said not to be silly, adding, "You may have saved our company, Custis! You may have noticed how many passengers we carry here to Rosebud Wash. If we get mail and maybe even passengers to deliver all the way to Fort Bidwell . . ."

"You likely will," he said. "As things now stand, dependents and soldiers on leave have a time getting *anywheres* from there. I told another blond lady she'd have to go on all the way to the coast to catch a train east. She seemed mighty vexed about it, too. Had there been a stage line in operation, then and there, I feel sure she'd have taken it."

Irene raised an eyebrow. "Oh? You certainly manage to meet a lot of *women* out in that desert, Custis."

He laughed. "Don't talk dirty. I never even kissed her." That was true enough, and he was still sore about it.

But he knew for a fact where he could kiss a buxom brunette right now. He looked around for a wall clock, didn't see any, but said, "Well, it's getting late, Miss Irene. So, as long as we're straight about my coach ticket and such . . ."

"Have some more coffee. There's so much you still have to tell me, Custis. It's not that late, and I'll never get a lick of sleep if you don't tell me how you and the colonel mean to catch up with those other Austrians!"

He settled back and put an arm up on the back of the sofa behind her. "The gal is only half-Austrian and I ain't sure she deserves to get sent back with old Krinke. She seems to be more politically confused than outright crooked. Hans Krinke printed up some stuff for her rebel outfit and, one thing leading to another when all concerned is young and healthy, she took up with him, convinced he's some sort of Robin Hood. Now *there's* a subversive book for you! Half the crooks I catch claim to be inspired by Robin Hood. Though I've yet to meet any poor people they've *given* all that much to."

Irene pouted. "You men are all alike when it comes to a no doubt well-upholstered redhead. I'll bet if *I* told whopping lies to the law I'd wind up in prison forever!"

Her shoulder was sort of bony, but he patted it reassuringly and told her, "I doubt that. You ain't all that ugly, Miss Irene. As to that other gal, I'm hoping she won't get caught. It's dumb to admire Karl Marx, but it ain't illegal. His fool movement will never amount to much."

"I heard he's an awful man who wants to turn the whole world upside down. If that redhead's on his side, she must be awful, too."

Longarm stared wistfully into the dark fireplace and mused aloud, "Oh, I dunno. She didn't strike me as really cruel-natured, just a mite excited. I still don't know how much of her act was a desperate attempt to save her boyfriend and how much might have been pure

166

enthusiasm for her cause. But let's forget her. Hans Krinke is the one we aim to send back to Vienna town."

"Don't you have to catch him first? After sending you and that Austrian lawman on such a wild-goose chase, he could be anywhere on earth by now, right?"

He chuckled and patted her shoulder again. "Not *anywhere* on earth. I doubt he'll ever return to Vienna town on his own. That narrows the search down some."

He noticed she didn't flinch when he touched her shoulder, so he left his hand there. But if he was wrong, it was getting late to see the bigger and softer Babs Westbury. Women asked such pesky questions when a man came calling after midnight that it was hardly worth the effort. He yawned, even though he wasn't sleepy, and said, "The colonel says he knows lots of Austro–Hungarians in Rye Patch. Maybe he does. I don't have to study on it before we get there, so I don't aim to. I got to study on finding me a place to bed down for the night."

She hesitated, blushed, and murmured, "If I let you stay here, just for the night, could I . . . trust you?"

"Nope. You're a handsome woman and I'm a man who's been out on the desert a spell, Miss Irene," he told her.

She giggled. "You're just joshing me. I guess I know what a skinny dishwater thing I am."

Longarm sensed she wasn't just fishing for compliments. He hauled her a shade closer and asked her, quietly, "Want to tell about it, pard?"

She almost but didn't pull away as she replied evasively, "Tell you about what? There's nothing to tell. It wasn't my fault I was born plain, damn it."

He said, "I've seen better-looking gals, no offense,

but you ain't that bad. You *knew* that, before someone *hurt* you, didn't you?"

She turned to stare up at him in wonder. "My Lord, you likely *will* catch up with that wanted foreigner. You don't miss much, do you?"

"Your problem ain't a federal offense, even though you likely think it should be, Miss Irene. Lots of borderline-pretty gals has been made to feel plain by some ornery cuss."

"How could you know about me and Roy? Nobody here in Rosebud Wash could have told you about the way he did me dirty!"

Longarm said, "Let me guess. After you got engaged it seemed only natural to go a mite further with your intended, right?'

She blushed beet-red.

He said, "I *said* it was only *natural*, Miss Irene. Some men will say anything to have their way with a young gal. So he did, and you did, and then he backed out on you. It left you hurt, with a chip on your heart and a pessimistic view of your mirror. You've been burying yourself in your work, letting your hair get stringy, and feeling you must have *failed*, some way. I'll tell you a secret. Some gents would walk out on *Cleopatra*, once they'd cashed in their chips with her. He was just a skunk."

Something broke behind her eyes and she was bawling like a baby in his arms. He patted her, saying, "There, there. It wasn't your fault, and you're still pretty, hear?"

She sobbed, "I loved him so, and I let him do such shocking things! I felt so low and soiled when he went back East without even saying goodbye!"

Longarm said, "I figured he'd had some experience at leaving his . . . ah . . . fiancées. How long's it been since he done you dirty, honey?"

She said, "Over a year, and I'm still hurting! You see, I'm ashamed to say it, but I *liked* it. Try as I might to hate him, I still can't help remembering how *good* it felt!"

He smiled. "I'd best be on my way, lest *I* start acting wicked, Miss Irene. But I want you to study on my parting words. It ain't low-down or soiled to crave what you've been craving. It's a scientific fact, writ down by Professor Darwin, that folks who don't enjoy it die out and don't leave no future family tree. He calls it Evolution."

"Pooh! I don't believe in that scandalous evolution nonsense. I was raised by the Good Book, Custis."

He chuckled. "I ain't up to arguing theology. I'm talking common sense. Both science and religion say it's only natural for men and women to enjoy slap and tickle. So stop feeling so sorry for yourself and get yourself another man to treat you right."

She sighed and asked, "In Rosebud Wash? I've *thought* about doing all them bad things with another man to get over Roy, Custis. But until tonight, I ain't had the *chance!*"

"Hold on, girl. I ain't no chance. I'm a stranger passing through. Come this time tomorrow, I'll be long gone."

She giggled. "I know. But whether you're forgotten as well or not, I'll still be *even* with that rascal Roy, won't I?"

"I come here to get a stagecoach ride, not to help you

169

get revenge, Miss Irene. Besides, you're sort of young and inexperienced, no offense, and . . ."

"He taught me how to take care of myself," she cut in, snuggling closer.

Longarm rolled his eyes heavenward and said, "Well, Lord, you can't say I didn't try!"

Then he picked her up, carried her to the four-poster, and began to undress her.

"Oh, what do you think you're *doing,* Custis?" she gasped.

He swore softly and replied, "This is a hell of a time to tell me I made a mistake, honey."

"Don't get sore. I *want* to be wicked with you. But do you have to take my *duds* off? I've never let a man see me *naked* before."

He sighed. "I thought you wanted some grown-up loving, not kid stuff in a hayloft. It's *better* with your duds off, honey. Trust me. I know what I'm doing, even if you don't."

She let him undress her, but she was trying to cover her breasts with her hands at the same time as he shucked his own things and took her in his naked arms.

He couldn't say if it was because he'd spent all those nights on the trail looking back on the Grover girls and forward to Babs Westbury, but they both sure had a grand old time.

Chapter 12

The stagecoach ride to Rye Patch was hot, dry, and dusty, and would have been tedious for Longarm even with someone prettier than Von Thaldorf seated across from him.

They got down feeling stiff in Rye Patch and headed for the railroad depot. The Austrian said something about tickets to San Francisco as they entered the cavernous waiting room. Longarm said, "We'll be going the other way. The redhead may have gone on to Frisco to wait for Krinke. But *he* ain't there, and I've chased all the wild geese I feel up to right now."

The other man asked what on earth he was talking about, unless he knew where Hans Krinke was. Longarm spotted two men coming their way in the gloom. "I ain't sure for *certain* where the rascal is," he said, "but we ought to know soon enough. That short, stubby gent is my boss, Marshal Vail. I wired him to meet us here. We'll know in a minute who that taller gray gent might be."

Billy Vail hailed them. "It's about time you got here, Longarm. I want you boys to meet Herr Oriskany from the Austro–Hungarian embassy. He got out here as soon as he could, and we met in Cheyenne. Is this Colonel Von Thaldorf?"

It wasn't. Whoever it was shoved Longarm one way and ran the other. Longarm didn't go down. He went after, shouting, "Give it up! You're caught, and it's too hot to play tag."

A porter was in the line of fire, so Longarm had to chase the imposter instead of dropping him the easy way with his drawn .44.

Two women were coming in as the fugitive reached the station entrance. He crashed into them and knocked both of them down. He tripped over a high-button shoe attached to a not-bad leg and, breaking stride, swung about to face Longarm with his own gun out.

There were times for sweet reason, and this was not one of them, so Longarm fired at the same time.

His aim was better. A dragoon ball just ruined the hanging gas lamp above his head, showering him with shards of frosted glass. The man in the doorway jerked like a puppet on a string and fell outside on the station walk. From the way his black Stetson fluttered down from on high to rest near the smoking dragoon inside the doorway, Longarm knew it had been a spine shot.

He moved to help the more shaken lady to her feet, saying, "I'm sure sorry, ma'am. I hope you ain't hurt."

Her less shaken companion sat up to stare out the doorway. "That man there must be!" she observed.

Longarm helped her up as well. "He ain't injured, ma'am," he told her. "He's killed. You ladies stay in here and don't look at him closer. I got to. It goes with the job."

By this time Billy Vail and the Austro–Hungarian official had joined them. Vail asked mildly, "How come you just gunned Colonel Von Thaldorf, old son?"

Longarm said, "I never. I didn't *think* he could be the real thing. But you'll note I held my fire till he bolted and proved I was right."

The three of them stepped out for a better look. Somewhere in the blazing sunlight a police whistle commenced to chirp. Both of the older men allowed they had never laid eyes on the dead man's blank face until shortly before. Longarm dropped to one knee, hooked a thumbnail under one edge of the realistic saber scar, and peeled it off. "I don't know what they call collodion in German," he explained. "But here in the U. S. it's used on minor cuts. If you ain't cut and put some on anyway, it puckers up the skin as it dries waterproof. He must have had a bottle of collodion in the shaving kit he fooled with at the oddest times. It should be in the baggage he dropped, yonder, when he decided to jackrabbit."

He tugged on the dead man's waxed moustache. "This is real. Reckon he planned ahead some. He sure was a *planning* cuss."

Oriskany still looked confused. "I can see he is not

173

my old comrade, Oberst Von Thaldorf. So who on earth *is* he?" he asked.

Longarm said, "If it ain't the colonel, it has to be the one and original Hans Krinke he was sent to arrest. There's nobody else left."

Vail gasped. "Damn it! Sorry, Ladies. You should have had him in cuffs, not fully armed, when you introduced him to us just now!"

"I never introduced him to nobody," Longarm said. "He bolted as soon as he saw I was *about* to introduce him to someone who might know he wasn't who he said he was. I wasn't sure till then. Not dead sure, leastways, and by any name he drawed as sweet. You'd have been even madder at me if I'd had to shoot it out with the one true guest of the U. S. government, wouldn't you?"

A blue-uniformed copper badge came along the walk to where he could see the cause of the disturbance better. As he slid to a stop Longarm called to him, "It's all right, pard. We're law, too, and this cuss on the walk wasn't. Could you keep a crowd from forming as we sort things out here?"

The copper couldn't, so Longarm led Vail and Oriskany inside so they could talk some more while the town of Rye Patch admired the cadaver in the doorway.

In the cooler waiting room, he explained, "Now that I know for sure what I only suspicioned before, this is how I suspect the tale can be told. The late Hans Krinke and his gal were making a grand tour of the West, trying to throw a dogged manhunter off their trail. The late Colonel Von Thaldorf was good. He wired us from Salt Lake when he tracked 'em that far. Remember, boss?"

Vail frowned and said, "He never mentioned female suspects of *any* description, old son."

Longarm reached for a smoke as he replied. "That could have been an oversight on the colonel's part or, like me, he saw no reason to get excited about side issues. The gal wasn't wanted by the law in Vienna town. She was just a warm-natured little thing, inclined to criticize the government, not an out-and-out crook like Krinke. I know for a fact she never carried lethal weapons."

He lit his cheroot and continued. "Krinke wouldn't have told her what a real villain he was. She had him down as some sort of romantic Robin Hood, persecuted by mean old Franz Josef. I doubt she was directly involved in the murder."

Oriskany gasped. "Murder? *Herr Gott,* who? Where?"

Longarm shrugged. "If the real Colonel Von Thaldorf trailed 'em as far west as Salt Lake, he'd be *around* here, somewhere, by now, if he was still alive. I figure Krinke somehow got the drop on him. He killed others pretty good, even when they was looking. Before he hid the body he helped himself to its I.D., recent communications, and such. So he had to know his victim had requested help and that help was on the way. At the same time, he could see the only American law he was apt to meet in the near future was a fool deputy who had no notion what *either* of 'em looked like."

Oriskany objected, "That man you just shot bears no resemblance at all to the real Oberst Von Thaldorf, Herr Long."

Longarm said, "I never went to military school with

either of 'em and, hell, how many Austrian accents with saber scars and waxed moustaches does your average U. S. deputy meet in a day? They was both the same mighty average size and build, so—"

Vail cut in, "Why would even a foreigner want to take such an awesome chance, Longarm? Why couldn't he have just gone on looking like his own self, once he murdered the only man west of the Big Muddy who knew him on sight?"

"He could have," Longarm said. "I'd have had a chore hunting for a man I'd never seen. But you know and he knew I'd likely *keep looking*, once I got this far and found no infernal Austrian lawman to meet me. There wasn't much he could do about his general appearance and accent. There ain't many folk of *any* description in these parts. So he knew he couldn't avoid passing interest, no matter which way he passed. Since hiding from me *total* would have been tough, he decided to keep me from hunting him down by offering to help me hunt him down. Nobody here in Nevada had ever seen the real colonel. It was easy enough for old Krinke to leave word here for me, as Von Thaldorf, saying he had a line on the Oregon-bound rascal, and so on. I might or might not have gone after him across the desert. Either way, he knew I'd wire you, as I did, that the notorious Hans Krinke was out there somewhere. The tale about a police informant here in Rye Patch was pure bull, of course. He just grabbed a stage to the end of the line, met up with a wagon train going father, and joined it to hunt like hell for his own fool self some more."

Longarm looked away to avoid Vail's keen gaze. "I got there later. His redhead caught up with me and added to the confusion by arguing politics nobody else connected to the case gave a hoot in hell about. But, whether by accident or design, she convinced me two Austrians instead of one was ahead of me out in that dust bowl. So, when I caught up with old Krinke, thinking he was someone else, at first, we had a swell time chasing nobody. I don't know how long we was supposed to hunt together before I agreed the rascal had given us the slip. That's why I wired for help in identifying my fellow lawman. It was getting tedious as hell."

Oriskany frowned and said, "It must have. But how long could the *schweinhund* have hoped to get away with such trickery?"

Longarm shrugged. "Long enough to leave us all confused beyond repair by the time you noticed your Colonel Von Thaldorf seemed to be missing, too. He had me weaving a mighty tangled web for him by sending all sort of messages putting the wanted Krinke where he couldn't be and the lawman after him where he'd never been. I noticed he didn't seem interested in contacting his own government. That's how I knew he wasn't likely to murder me as well. I was too *useful* to him as a dumb but willing dupe. He made a feeble attempt to ditch me in Rosebud Wash. When I took the same stage, anyway, he likely figured he had plenty of time and opportunity to drop off any old train, any old time and place. You see, I never told him you two would be here."

Vail stared at the crowded doorway and observed, "That did seem to upset him some. But I'm still missing something, Longarm. How did you get on to him if he was such a slick actor?"

Longarm said, "I don't know how good he could act.

I wouldn't know a real aristocrat from a fair-educated foreigner, in any case. I didn't have to act, much. He just took me for a natural fool as well as less refined."

Vail said, "I know you don't act sissy, Longarm. Get to what he done to give his *own* sissy self away!"

"He never, directly. He acted a mite stuck-up and surly for my taste, but that could have gone with a real saber scar and field grade commission. What gave him away as the fake colonel was the way the man we were supposed to be hunting together was acting. It's a simple fact of nature that when a man can't be there, it's safe to assume he ain't."

The two older men exchanged wary glances.

Longarm insisted, "Look, the only ones saying for sure that Krinke had passed through Rosebud Wash ahead of us was exactly two foreigners. Not a soul who *belonged* there could recall more than *one* gent from Vienna town passing through. And the town of Rosebud Wash was so small and nosy that I occasioned comment when I dropped out of sight long enough to enjoy a shower bath. They spotted me. They spotted the man calling his fool self Von Thaldorf. So how had *Krinke* got in or out?"

He took a drag on his cheroot and let out smoke expansively. "It pays to keep an open mind. So I let that go as I chased after the wagon train and caught up with the imposter. He said Krinke was somewhere out ahead of us in the desert. All right. I *said* I was open-minded. I scouted for sign as we continued all the infernal way to Fort Bidwell, slow. There wasn't none. Not a hoof or heel mark, even on bare dust. A man has to stop and camp at least once in a while."

178

Vail asked, "Couldn't such a desperate character take another trail, old son?"

Longarm looked disgusted. "We was on one that was so bad it was killing the emigrants by the time I caught up with 'em. I failed to see how a greenhorn could have found another, better or worse, in country he couldn't know better than me. He had to make it to water at least once every seventy-two hours. Water fit for man and beast to drink, I mean. I found it mysterious when a man who couldn't know too much about the desert managed to avoid dangerous sweetwater that could have fooled *me*, had not friendly Indians tipped me off ahead of time.

"It went from mysterious to impossible when I was asked to believe a dude, alone, had made it past a gang of armed toughs at another water hole. I had other things to worry about as well. I held my peace till we finally made Fort Bidwell and made sure nobody answering Krinke's description had. That's when I sent the wire asking you to meet me here with someone who knew Von Thaldorf at least. I slickered him into coming back by acting dumb about the redhead in the colonel's police dossier. The rest you know.

"Now I'd best have a word about that corpse out front with the local law. They can put him on ice or just take a photograph to send to Vienna town. The Salt Lake police would be the best to ask about the missing colonel. It's high summer, and he might not be hid too deep."

Oriskany looked sort of sick. He sat down on a waiting room bench as Longarm turned away.

Vail followed, caught his deputy's sleeve, and murmured, "Hold on, old son. What about that *redhead* that's still at large?"

Longarm said, "I was hoping you wouldn't ask that, Billy. She ain't wanted serious in Vienna town, and she ain't done nothing serious on *our* side of the pond. By now she could be most anywhere, black-headed, as well as scared more honest. I'd just as soon not go after her, if it was all the same to you."

Vail frowned thoughtfully. "Right. You went and compromised yourself as the arresting officer, again. *I* don't want to explain that to the department, neither. But do I have your word you won't get in any more trouble before I can get you on the evening train to Denver, you rascal?"

Longarm nodded. "Sure. There's a steam bath and a barber just up the street. Once I settle with the local law, I'll likely kill the rest of the time getting clean again. A man just never knows who he might meet aboard a night train, Billy."

Vail swore, laughed despite himself, and said, "I'd fire you for disgracing the department so often, if you wasn't so often so good. What makes you so horny, old son?"

Longarm looked innocent and replied, "Suffering snakes, Billy, can't you see I just come in from the wide and lonesome wilderness?"

Watch for

LONGARM AND THE RUNAWAY THIEVES

ninety-fourth novel in the bold
LONGARM series from Jove

coming in October!

LONGARM

Explore the exciting Old West with one of the men who made it wild!

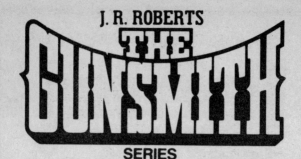

J. R. ROBERTS
THE GUNSMITH
SERIES